AFTER THE NOVA

An anthology by YA Stories

After the Nova
© 2021. YA Stories. All rights reserved.
Contributions have been made by: Lily Segna, Sophia Stecker, Isla Granger, Emma Le Breton, Midori Mehandjiysky, Aida Broshar, Tealia Jud, Dora Graham, Monika Jozic, Cana Severson, Alfredo Roman Jordan, Jordan Hines, Nicholas Hull, Laurel Childress, Annaliese Ai Gumboc, Abigail M. Hull, Camille S. Campbell, Katelyn Crombie

Published in the United States by the Unapologetic Voice House. The Unapologetic Voice House is a hybrid publishing house focused on publishing strong female voices and stories.
www.theunapologeticvoicehouse.com

Paperback ISBN: 978-1-955090-18-6
Ebook ISBN: 978-1-955090-19-3
Library of Congress Control Number: 2021949874

Contents

Foreword

BEING A TEENAGER IS ONE OF THE MOST THRILLING EXPERIences in the world. Before your eyes, the dreamscapes of your childhood are bolstered by new people, places, and experiences. Youthful hunger is set free to the wide-open world, and you'll find that there are endless spectacles to behold. In the years between your elementary and high school graduations, you'll uncover many truths about yourself, and you'll discover so many passions. It's a vivid period of your life.

But your teenage years can also be incredibly hard. As you shoulder more responsibilities, you'll feel like both a child and an adult, and you'll be treated like both at once. You're given agency in some respects, and yet you're restricted in other freedoms. It can be contradictory, confusing, and frustrating. And you may find yourself struggling with things that you don't have words to express.

I thought that my high school experience would be dictated by classes and college decisions; dates and drama; homecoming and hijinks, and to a degree, it was. I learned so much about myself, and I had a ton of fun along the way. But to be frank, many in my peer group struggled with mental illness in high school. Teenagers today are living through a mental health epidemic, where approximately one in five teens in the United States are living with a diagnosable mental health disorder. Human existence can be hard, and in this time period when you want to handle everything by yourself, it can be even harder to accept that you're not okay. Many of us feel isolated and attempt to shoulder our burdens alone. However, one of the biggest lessons of your teenage years is that accepting support is a sign of strength, not weakness.

This is why I chose the themes of mental health and self-reliance for our anthology. In recent years with the pandemic, it has felt like we are living in a dystopian world. These short stories are written in the genre of science fiction, and their settings span mountains, oceans, and the stars. But what they all hold in common is a tenacity of spirit in the face of adversity—something that the youth of today have demonstrated many times over. As an older member of Generation Z myself, I wanted to help pave the way for those who come after me, creating the channels to help their voices be heard. That is the mission of YA Stories—to amplify the voices of the young and to share their insights with the world. And you'll find that these contributors possess a nuance and a sharpness of wit as strong as any author. We often underestimate the keenness of youth, but these stories are riveting all the while unveiling human truths.

To the writers who contributed their stories to this anthology: thank you. We cherish your spirit, ingenuity, and your craft. Your stories make a difference. Your voice matters. You are heard.

Hannah Weinberg, 20
YA Stories Coordinator

BY KATELYN CROMBIE, 16

A Chance at Tomorrow

LILY SEGNA, 15

TWO WEEKS PRIOR, THE CONDEMNING LETTER HAD BEEN LEFT in the arena. It had been addressed to no one, but meant for her.

I know who you are and why you hide the letter read.

Three pages long, the letter had gone on to describe every detail of the identity she'd fought so hard to hide, because to reveal her identity was to forfeit her life.

And because of the blackmail letter (how in the *world* had they figured out her identity?), Shou had been forced into a high-stakes fight against the arena's current champion—who didn't know the reason for the fight—the winner of which would become weapons master. As the current weapons master, Shou had everything to lose. The coveted position and the protection of her identity were the only things keeping her alive.

The fight was in mere hours. Her opponent was a hulking giant of a man who called himself Slammer.

His weapon of choice was the *biggest* double-bladed axe that Shou—or anyone, for that matter—had ever seen. In stark contrast, Shou's weapons of choice required far more finesse: an arm-length extender staff that snapped out to nearly two meters in length and a set of duo cirades, two circular blades used in a style almost mimicking a pair of curved swords.

Every bit of Shou's appearance was as much for show as functionality—designed to make her appear stronger and bigger—especially the mask, which altered her voice and hid her entire face from judgmental audiences.

Hopefully, the theatrics would confuse Slammer's pebble of a brain.

Time was ticking. Every second was one closer to the fights. Already, spectators and fighters alike had begun trickling through the doors and taking seats in the arena, whispering eagerly about the fights to come. As soon as the rickety stands were full and the fighters accounted for, Shou signaled for the fights to begin.

The first fight was between a tall beanpole of a woman named Enif and a young man who went by Kickback. It was not a fair fight. Kickback had at least thirty years of youth over Enif, five times the muscle and was considered one of the arena's best fighters. The fight was over in a matter of minutes with Kickback emerging on top.

Suddenly there were only seven fights before Shou's. Then there were six.

Five.

Four.

The night was rushing by.

Three.

Two.

The fight before Shou's was over far too soon and out of nowhere, it was time for her to face Slammer. Taking a deep breath, the five-foot, hundred pound girl headed down to the arena floor and prepared to face off against the seven-foot, three hundred pound brute of a man.

Slammer was waiting for her, cracking his knuckles with a ferocity that made Shou think he was going to break his hands before the fight even started, though it wouldn't have upset her if he did. "Let's raise the stakes, shall we?" He swung his axe around a few times too, just for good measure, and pointed it at her with a cocky air. "I win, you remove the mask. You win, you keep it on."

Under her mask, Shou inhaled sharply. *No, no, no.* Why did he care? Did he suspect who she was?

The crowd jeered, shouting taunts down at her.

After a moment, she relented. Protesting would only make it worse. "You win, I remove the mask." She let the corner of her mouth turn up into a lopsided grin that no one could see. "*I* win, I get the axe."

The whole arena fell silent. No one had expected *that*.

Slammer weighed his axe in his hand, gazing down at it. Finally he narrowed his eyes. "Deal." Without further ado, he hurled his axe at Shou's head. She barely had a split second to duck out of the way.

He charged, ramming into her and throwing her head over heels across the arena. She was pretty sure the noise from the impact had been audible from kilometers away. There was no time to find out, because Slammer was stampeding towards her again.

This time, Shou was slightly more prepared and rolled out of the way, reaching out with her extender to trip Slammer. He hit the ground, his momentum propelling him across the arena. Unfortunately for Shou, he skidded to a halt next to his axe and thundered back over to swing it at her head. Shou's extender hit the axe, deflecting it. Huffing out a breath, she pushed back to her feet, dancing away from Slammer's next blow.

Before she could retaliate with a blow of her own, Slammer smacked her with the flat side of the axe. Shou collapsed, head crashing against the ground. Her vision blurred. It took her a moment to get up.

"It's that it?" Slammer bellowed. "You fight like a *girl*." The crowd roared with laughter.

Shou winced, the remark hitting too close to home. She sent him a rude gesture with her left hand as she simultaneously jabbed the extender at his chest with her right hand. She parried the next blow and the next, until she saw an opening. Dashing forward, Shou whirled under Slammer's guard and stabbed the blade of her extender into his chest. Turning away, Slammer twisted the extender out of her grip and flung it across the arena, growling down at his bleeding chest.

Shou was left disarmed, albeit the cirades at her belt. She was panting, exhausted. A bead of sweat rolled down her forehead, but she ignored it and grinned to herself. "Is that it?" she drawled. "I thought you were better than this." Slammer growled, an inhuman sound. "Come on," Shou taunted, bouncing on her toes as if that would make her exhaustion go away faster. "Do your worst."

With his right hand, Slammer threw a punch that Shou deftly dodged—only to come face-to-face with the hulking brute's other fist. He flung her against the far wall.

SMACK.

Slammer did his worst.

Her vision blurred, her mind went fuzzy and she had a moment of panic in which she could not remember where she was or why she was there, all of which were telltale signs of a severe concussion. It took her a couple heartbeats to remember the fight, and in that time, she took in a long breath and surveyed the arena. Every onlooker in the crowd had a spectral double, and the walls were spinning.

The walls were not supposed to spin. *Or were they?*

A shadowy monster made its way into her vision and pointed an oddly shaped object at her. It took a moment for Shou to realize the monster was Slammer and the object was his axe. The crowd booed.

"You've lost," boomed Slammer's voice. Shou winced. No, she hadn't lost. Not yet. Pushing herself up, she fumbled for the cirades at her sides, tugged one free, and flung the weapon at Slammer. He frowned and stepped back to avoid it. Once it was past him, Shou held her hand out. The trackers in the cirade activated, flying back to her and slicing a cut across Slammer's arm. *Success.* She threw the cirade again, but this time, Slammer caught the blade's grip and tossed it away, striking her down with the flat side of his axe. Shou fell back.

"Get *up!*" someone in the crowd yelled. "*Get up!*"

With some difficulty, she managed to kneel and hold out her last cirade in both hands, pointing it shakily at Slammer. He knocked it away and kicked her down. Again.

"*Get up!*"

Shou couldn't.

"GET UP!"

It was too hard.

"GET. *UP!*"

The walls were spinning, the noise from the crowd was thunder, her head was pounding, and she couldn't. *Get up, you idiot, get up.*

The announcer made the proclamation. "*And* the fight goes to Slammer. Congratulations to our new weapons master!"

Lost. I've lost.

The crowd went wild. *Slammer! Slammer!* Slammer flung his axe into the ground and threw his arms up, shouting triumphantly along with the crowd. After a moment of victorious cheering, he reached over and yanked off Shou's mask. Her hair tumbled down in layers around her shoulders, reminiscent of a curtain.

The arena fell dead silent, quieter than it had ever been.

"A *girl*," Slammer said finally, as if being one was the worst crime imaginable. As if he didn't notice anything else about her identity. Someone in the crowd made the connection to Slammer's earlier taunt, the one about Shou fighting like a girl, and shouted it out. Disgusted, Slammer flung the mask down at her feet. Shou picked it up unsteadily. She felt oddly vulnerable without it, not to mention that everyone in the arena could see the golden-brown eyes that marked her as the heir to a long-since persecuted bloodline. She was as good as dead.

Slammer grunted in disgust, reclaimed his axe and stomped off into the crowd of spectators, who quickly followed suit.

Shou found the wall and slumped against it, the world still spinning around her. Over the pounding in her head, she heard the crunch of footsteps. Cursing the concussion for addling her brain, Shou hoped it wasn't someone approaching with malicious intent. There wouldn't be much she could do to defend herself.

Through unfocused eyes, she saw two men. Both were weaponless, which—to some extent—relieved Shou.

As they approached, she realized the taller one was Kickback, the fighter from the first match. The other man was a stranger. He held up his hands, palms out. "We mean you no harm."

"Good," said Shou, running her fingertips bitterly across the ridges of her mask. "Now go away."

Kickback frowned. His spectral double, a vision induced by Shou's concussion, frowned too.

The other man gave him a pointed look. "You fought well," he tilted his head to Shou, "but lost *everything*. You have potential. All you need is some focused training."

"So?" Shou retorted. Training didn't matter. More fighting was *not* going to be a part of her future, if that's what he was suggesting.

The man relented, crossing his arms. "You're small and cunning; you'll be able to get past people unnoticed. You would probably make a good spy, and you know your way around a fight." He gave a nonchalant shrug. "There's an open position on our crew. Above-world. You have all the skills we're looking for and with your lineage....well, nobody messes with one of ours. You in?" An invitation was the only way to join a crew. And she'd just been invited. She caught her breath. Most crews worked underworld in the black market, but a select few—known as above-world *crews*—worked to save lives instead of take them: stopping terrorists, fighting crime. Things that would make the world a better place.

It didn't take much consideration. Shou wanted more to her life, and this was an opportunity she had previously only dreamed of having. Add in the benefit of protection and there was no way she was turning this down.

"Yes," she said. "I'm in." She let out a long breath, shook out her wrists, rolled back her shoulders and felt herself truly unwind for what felt like the first time in years. It felt good.

"Excellent," the man held out his hand to her. She took it shakily, still seeing double. He helped her stand. "Let's go."

Shou cast one last look around the arena, a small smile drifting across her mouth at what had been her entire existence. But not anymore. She exhaled again and let it all go. She had a future to attend to, and she never planned to step foot in this arena ever again.

And though there were mere hours remaining until daybreak, Shou would take the sleep she could. In the morning, she'd get up, and though there was never really any guarantee of survival, she would at least have a chance at tomorrow.

Imperfect

SOPHIA STECKER, 15

A S FAR AS THE EYE CAN SEE, THE FIELDS ARE SPECKLED RED. The Fumeum flowers are blooming. I grab another flower by the stalk and add it to my basket. My abraded hands sting in the morning chill. Harvest season has come early this year. All around me, strips of blossoms stretch out into the distance.

Up in the dark sky, stars glow brightly through the thin atmosphere. The planet we orbit, Ocelos, is visible in all its green glory. Around that patch of paradise, the void of space stretches, endless, empty, and cold.

My throat closes up and I look down. A cold feeling spreads in my chest. With that *thing* looking at me all hours of the day, it's hard to forget I'm on a tiny moon, hurtling through space, miles and miles and miles and miles away from the next closest inhabited solar system.

Come on Jacey, think of something else, I say to myself. I'm not going to get scared today. Today is supposed to be different. My heart quickens its tempo and my mind

15

fixes onto all the things that I'm not supposed to think about. Like how there's no air in space, how it's freezing, and anyone exposed directly to it would die instantly. Like how eventually our star will explode, and maybe someday every star will explode, and the universe will be cold and dark and empty. I resist the urge to curl up on the ground.

At least I'm alone. At least no one can see the way my mouth curls into a grimace, the way I drop my Fumeum basket and squeeze my eyes shut. At least no one will see my fear.

At least no one will realize.

I retrieve my basket and begin yanking up the Fumeum with renewed vigor. With each flower, I shove my rebellious thoughts deeper into my skull. My heart's hammering subsides, but a sense of unease remains.

One of the flower's petals rips and I bite back an exclamation. I need all the Fumeum I can get. An imperfect blossom isn't good enough for the garlands off-planet buyers are looking for. The flower's beautiful face beams up at me, undiminished by the tear. I slip it into a pocket. On this moon, more Fumeum means more money, and with no family, I'm all I've got. I glance at my flower basket. Considering how much people on Ocelos are willing to pay for a bouquet of Fumeum, my wage is laughable.

Given the choice, I would leave this moon, this job, in an instant, but there isn't a choice. Ocelos won't let any of the lunar citizens leave. We're too valuable to their economy. But that was never enough to keep us down. Everyone on this moon is scrambling for any chance to get away, but I just might be the closest to that dream. My best friend works in the space docks, and we've been plotting to steal a ship for months. It doesn't seem quite real though. I guess I don't believe that escape is achievable. I'm trapped. On a rock, flying through space, surrounded by the endless sea of the cold, dark void. I train my eyes on my flowers. On their scarlet petals and perfect leaves.

I'll have to give them away at the end of the day. They'll be packed into containers and loaded aboard a transport ship. And then they'll be launched into space, with only the walls of the transport between them and the endless vacuum.

Only a call from across the fields prevents my thoughts from spiraling again. I turn my head, shielding my eyes from the rising sun. Running through the fumeum flowers comes a short girl with a curly head of hair tied up with a red ribbon. Alice. My best friend.

She runs up to me grinning, her umber eyes bright. Her face is deep bronze, slightly flushed from exertion. She grabs me by my shoulders and laughs.

"Jacey, I've done it! I figured out how to get us a ship, but we need to go *now.*" she whispers.

I open my mouth, but nothing comes out.

I swallow hard. Escape. We can get out of here. Though I've been here my whole life, it's never felt like home. Alice is the only person I'd call family, and now the two of us can *leave*. The concept seems alien, impossible, utterly unachievable, and even now I don't quite believe we can do it. Still, Alice is the smartest, most ingenious person I know. If she says we can do it, we can. "Alright Alice. Lead the way."

Her face lights up. She pivots, feet etching holes in the soft earth, and half carries me away. We race through the flowers, and for a time all there is in the world is us and the rows upon rows of Fumeum. I'm lifted up by the heady scent of the flowers and the humid air they thrive in. Maybe we really can escape. Maybe I'll be able to step onto a spaceship and ride all the way to freedom without letting my fear slip out, my mask slip. Without the person I admire most in the world realizing I'm a coward.

And then that pleasant fantasy is shattered. Gleaming metal looms out over the red flowers. A monumental building stretches up into the sky. "The hanger," Alice says. I can already feel my heart rate begin to elevate. "Everyone will be back from break soon, so we have to hurry."

I grab her arm. "Hold on Alice, what if someone sees us?"

"Most of the personnel are on break, and I know the places to avoid."

"And then," I swallow, "and then we'll have to get on a ship? Are you sure it's safe?"

I can't quite read Alice's expression as she says, "Perfectly. But don't think about that right now. First we have to get in."

She rushes us into a side door and through sterile white hallways. The smell of cleaning product mixed with fuel hangs in the air. Alice pushes me into an elevator, and I watch the floor number over the top of the door go up and up and up and up, closer and closer to... then the entirety of what we're about to do hits me.

We are going to steal a ship. We are going to fly that ship into outer space all the way to an interstellar gate that will transport us to another other corner of the galaxy. *Space.* The empty lonely void where nothing lives and nothing exists except giant burning stars light-years away from each other. My palms clam up and my mouth twists and suddenly my body's working overtime, pumping me full of adrenaline, and I'm breathing so fast I feel light headed, and *my god I can't do this.*

I can't do this.

Make it stop.

Someone grabs my shoulder. I hear Alice's voice in my ear. She says something, but it sounds like it's coming from the end of a long tunnel. I start to speak but my voice sounds so frenzied that I clamp my jaw shut. She will not see me like this. Alice puts her arm around me and we stand in silence.

Then the elevator dings, the door opens, and I'm surrounded by spaceships. Looming, sleek shapes in all colors. The room stretches on forever, but there is no sound, no other living thing besides us as we weave between the sleeping giants. It would be beautiful if it wasn't so terrifying. The ceiling hangs high, high above us, and I catch glimpses of passenger vessels, rich people's luxury ships, and even a long white embassy craft with the Ocelos emblem printed on the side. But Alice walks past all of these beautiful, safe looking spaceships without a second glance and leads me over to an empty Fumeum transport. Its rickety frame and peeling paint send my heart into my throat. Alice steps into the cockpit and starts messing with the controls.

My voice is barely a whisper as I ask, "Alice? Alice why are we taking this ship, please, can we take something safer?"

She glances up, seeming not to understand how horrifying her choice is. "They'll notice if we steal one of the flashier ships, but this girl?" She pats the dash affectionately. "I doubt anyone will miss her." She grins at me. How can she be so calm? "We do need to hurry though. Hop in."

I can't make myself move. I could let her leave by herself, but then I'm stuck in the fields and my best friend is gone forever. But the other option, to go to space...

I can't do this.

I can feel Alice's eyes fixed on my face. "Something's wrong. You're scared."

"I'm not scared," I say faintly.

"Jacey, what's wrong?"

My mouth refuses to work for several seconds, and then it all comes rushing out. "I–I've put off telling you this for a while. The thing is, I'm afraid. Of space. Whenever I think about it too much, I freeze up. It's dangerous and cold, and–god Alice, I can't do this. I want to leave, but I think you're going to have to go without me." My insides feel all twisted up. "Please don't think I'm pathetic."

She's absolutely silent for a few seconds, and then she says, "Jacey, I know. I thought... I'm sorry, I thought we were pretending I didn't notice. And you're not pathetic. You know that."

I finally drag my eyes from the floor and back to her. "But it's irrational. I know up here," I gesture to my head, "that we'll be safe in that ship and nothing bad will happen, and the longer I keep you here, the closer we are to being caught. But I'm still scared, and that's stupid."

Over the intercom, I hear a garbled voice telling the personnel to return to their posts, and I know our time is up; I have to choose now.

Alice shoots a frenzied glare at the elevator but keeps the ship's door open for me. She leans over the edge of the cockpit and looks me dead in the eye. "All right, here it is. We need to leave now if we're leaving at all, but I'm not going if you're not."

I stare at her in shock. It's too much. Alice, the intercom, space. Stay, get caught, and leave. Too many thoughts and too little time, and I have to *choose, choose, choose—*

Wait.

What do I *want*? Did I ever consider that?

And then I climb into the cockpit.

I'm still half drowned in terror, and my brain is screaming at me to stay away, but I choose me. I choose freedom. My hand finds the little red flower in my pocket. The one with the tear. It's not perfect, but its imperfections don't make it lesser. They make it beautiful.

And even though I'm so, so scared, I know we're going to do great things.

Danger Fish

ISLA GRANGER, 13

October 10

Water. Water was all I've seen for months. You'd think only seeing water for a few days would be good, but not for me because I've been stuck in the ocean forever

Kai is making me write in this notebook thing because they think it'll be good for me. What am I even going to write about? This amazing blue water? Anyways I guess I'm going to write out the current situation so if we ever find land I can turn this into a book and publish it. Basically we are stuck on this tiny triangle shaped boat. Me, Kai, and Michael are trying to find land, but we have two problems with this plan. First problem, and also the cause of this predicament is the government, because it collapsed. Riots were happening. All in all it was the government against the people which led to genetic mutation, which of course didn't really do much.

What did do much was the radioactive power plant. Because it was being over used, it exploded leaving a huge radius of bad areas. Half of this area being ocean. The fish got accidentally genetically mutated, which to our disadvantage got bigger and more viscous.

Problem number two, because we can't touch or get in the water (because of the giant man eating fish) we're going slow, very, very slow. So now in this boat we randomly found, I'm writing in this notebook. Kai was being stubborn about this notebook thing but I guess it can't be that bad. It gives me something to do besides solve the puzzle book I found.

October 11

I'm here again. Michael was exploring the boat more. He found a cactus. He got pretty excited. It's fun to have him as a friend. He seems to balance out the sarcasm me and Kai are more fluent in. Like seriously both of them are complete opposites. I'm in the happy middle and possess a little bit of both of them. Michael is so chaotic and cheerful while Kai is lovingly sarcastic. Sometimes I wonder how the three of us became friends in the first place. Michael's appearance matches his personality perfectly, his dark skin and bouncy hair always seem to capture his bouncy and smiling personality. As I'm writing this Kai is watching me, so I am going write about them later. Anyways we haven't made much progress on our search for land. I can't say I miss society much because it went to waste but out here isn't much better, at least the boat we found had stuff in it. Kai seemed excited to search the boat at first but recently they don't seem as interested as before, they seem to have lost interest in most things as of recently, anyways their gone so I can write about them now. Kai is kinda the parent of me and Michael. They are the most reasonable and responsible out all of us. They're tiny size and rosy skin seem to show that enough.

October 14

I was talking to Kai. They said I should write about myself in case all of us don't make it out of here, so this is it I guess. My name is Alice and I'm a chubby person with brownish- orange hair. Kai insists I'm a redhead but I guess we'll never come to an agreement on that matter haha. I'm pretty extroverted and like to play soccer. Although sometimes it annoys me when I tell people I like sports and then immediately assume I'm lying because I'm kinda cubby. Anyways I noticed the birds are all mutated. I'll keep it to myself though. I wonder what I'd be doing right now if we didn't hop on this boat. Welp I gotta go help Michael and Kai (mostly Kai, they like to keep things tidy) clean the inside of this tiny ship.

October 16

Kai suggested another idea of something to write about. They said I should try to write about what we do each day, then Michael heard us and jumped in saying it was great idea. I guess I'll start by explaining the layout of the boat. It's an okay sized boat with two main areas. The deck and the inside. The deck doesn't have much on it. It's where we found most of the supplies. They were in the crates that littered the boat. There's a big crate in at the tip of the boat. The inside of the boat we used some rugs to make sleeping areas. At first we all slept in a giant pile but after a few days we all adopted corners. The extra corner almost like a living room. The day at this point usually goes as Michael wakes up and then accidentally wakes all of us up. Then we try to make a makeshift breakfast and then sit around and talk or I do my puzzle book sometimes. Around lunch time we go outside and try to get some sunlight and just keep a look out, then we go back inside make some dinner, and talk some more. Michael made a paper craft yesterday after dinner. We skip lunch to ration food, none of us have any idea how long we'll be here.

October 31

Today is Halloween if things were normal. I remember trick or treating with my family as a kid. Thinking back on those times makes me sad but those moments are important to remember. In an attempt to have some fun we playing hide and seek in the dark, like children. I was hiding behind an empty crate at the tip of the boat (where it curves up and where I sit and look for land). Kai was seeking and I thought I saw Michael run into the inside of the boat but I don't know if he was in there the whole time. I could hear Kai walking around behind me, probably checking in the other crates. Lucky for me I'm sure they couldn't see me because the crate I was hiding behind was big, even though I didn't have much space to curl up into on the boat the crate covered me well. I could hear Kai getting closer and was trying to get smaller when I heard it, bubbling from the water, I knew what that meant. I froze in fear, the seconds went by and nothing happened. I was sure I was safe so I started to try and get small again, then I heard it before I saw it. A crunching noise. Almost instinctively, I stood up and jumped back on the crate. I stared at the giant fish that had just bit in to the tip of the boat. Its eyes were fixed on me, staring, non-blinking. We made eye contact. Its body was a teal-grey color and its teeth were probably as long as my finger. It seemed to have realized its chance to turn me into dinner was gone and angrily swam away. After I got over the shock of the whole thing I slowly looked around and Kai standing there with a horrid expression on their face, they were beyond angry. I could tell. Then in short, they started screaming at me. It was kind weird to hear and see them so angry, it felt unreal.

"Why would you do something so dangerous? What if you just died and I lost someone in this already small party? Then what would I do?"

So in short the other day was less than fun, although after the screaming had stopped Michael jumped out of the inside of the ship because it had been too long and nobody had found him. It made me wonder how he could so easily give up on a game.

November 15

Sorry I haven't written as much lately, moving around and doing extra stuff takes more energy than ever it seems. After Kai snapped at me they've become more irritable and sarcastic and even Michael's halfhearted attempts to cheer them up don't work. They mostly just sleep and do minimal things. Even Michael seems down lately. I think the reality of this situation might have finally sunk in all the way. Now his chaos just seems to bother him instead of adding to his usually much more joyful personality. The entertainment is running low and so is the book of puzzles I found on the first day we got stuck here.

November 16

I'm going to try to be positive and write in this more. I'm glad that there was so much canned food in this boat, Michael suggested we should try to go fishing to save the canned goods and then did a face palm, that was pretty funny. I saw a normal bird today and pointed it out to everyone but nobody seemed super ecstatic about it, even Michael cheers seemed forced, Kai just scoffed, I'm pretty sure they don't think we're ever getting out of here, sometimes I agree, the situation just seems hopeless.

December 1

Michael seems to be trying to hide the fact that he's losing hope with halfhearted smiles and fake optimism. He was doing a good job at first but I think he's getting too tired to try hard at this point. I think he also misses his family, maybe even more than me. I'm starting to think I'm getting paranoid about the fish in the water, each time to see the bubbling in the water my brain immediately thinks about the big teal-grey fish that tried to bite me in half, I don't like going anywhere near the water now. I don't think this book will ever be published.

December 3

Kai yelled at Michael today and threw out his cactus. It was hard to watch, neither of them deserved it, I heard Kai cry later in the night, they didn't want to yell at him. By this point nobody really talks to each other, Kai isolated themself a few weeks ago and I don't leave my bed much which means I'm talking to Michael less and less. I saw another unmutated bird today. At least that was enough to give me some hope. I still miss life before this. It always seemed so bright. I'm sad I'm spending my time like this. I wish I could be more optimistic about myself. I used to have more confidence in myself in all ways but it just hasn't been here lately

December 12

I've seen a few unmutated birds this week and the fish seem to be becoming less and less threatening. I'm the only one who really seems to care though, at least it's something. These passages are getting short but I'm running out of pages and there isn't much to talk about.

December 16

I've been talking to Michael more and even pointed out the birds and fish to him, he seemed glad, I'm happy there's at least a little more life in his eyes now.

January 2

I think me and Michael excitement is sinking into Kai, I've seen them twice in the last week.

January 5

Land! I saw land on the horizon and I showed Michael and Kai, now that the fish aren't really trying to kill us we can attempt to paddle to the faint land ahead of us.

January 6

This is the last day I'm writing in this book, even Michael and Kai talk to each other now, although Kai is still struggling with motivation to do things. Michael even got the spring in his step back and Kai got up twice today. I wonder if I'll find my family again, I've been wanting to see them for awhile. I probably shouldn't get my hopes up, but I really miss them (and hot meals). I think this book may be published after all!

Immortal Dust

EMMA LE BRETON, 15

T HE DAY THE WAR ENDS, FOG IS EVERYWHERE. IT'S IN THE
streets, strangling the city; it's up the river, fooling
children into approaching the deep end; it's on the
bridge and in every corner of the city, even in the slums,
suffocating the proletariat who whisper secrets to the
conspiring wind, who linger and lurk in packs in the
murk of the morning.

San is set to meet Leicester at the Dispensary tonight
for drinks. She leaves work just as the snow begins to
dwindle. Mixed with soot from chimneys, dust, and
mud from, well, everywhere, it gives birth to the city's
abominable interpretation of quicksand. They call it
quicksnow, and it looks like a large bruise on the ground.
If you step in the wrong spot, you lose your boot. (And
you certainly can't afford another.)

San is nearly done traipsing through quicksnow
when someone bursts out of the barter house, hollering
from the top of his lungs.

"WE WON!"

She whips her head up, but the man has already disappeared into the fog. Good. What a weirdo. Now all she sees in the square is that hideous statue of Cordovan "Cordo" Kyoul, whose only great talking point—if he were alive, that is—would be that time he accidentally blew himself up.

Cordo was the leader of one of the Scissor's subdivisions. He led a raid in one of the Opposition hospitals and met his fate stepping on an abandoned landmine.

Good for him. No one liked him anyway.

But somehow one of his Scissor chumps managed to erect his statue, here, right by the slums, so that all the starving Opposition members can stare at it and be reminded of where they truly belong. That's where all their tax money goes, but San can't exactly argue, can she? The Scissors *are* the government, and they see *everything*.

Exhibit A: there's a camera embedded in Cordo's left foot.

San shivers, and checks her watch. She's late.

She reaches the pub. Her outstretched hand, thin, grimy, tremors by the handle. She almost pulls back, not quite knowing why. Then cold metal bites her skin. San snaps out of her trance, gathers her few remaining wits, and goes in. A chorus of rowdy voices suddenly quiets down as all eyes turn to her.

Self-conscious, San coughs, and looks around. Leicester is at the bar, nursing a glass of sake–which is odd, because he only ever drinks beer.

She pulls a stool out. It screeches against the floor like a banshee. She huffs, hoping to disguise her embarrassment for irritation, and sits down.

Leicester stares.

"What?" she asks.

"My god..." he mumbles, his drink forgotten (a first, for him). "Have you not heard?"

"Heard what?"

"You- Oh, San. Not here."

He steers San outside, and points to the crates. "You'd better sit."

"Is it just me, or is everyone looking at me kind of funny? Like I'm Cordo's ghost."

"Take a breath, Sannie." He hands her the sake. "Drink."

She does. It tastes like lingo berry juice on steroids; but then again, how would she know? She hasn't had manufactured juice since she was five. It's too expensive. This drink is as close as she'll ever get.

"What's going on, Lee? Why is everyone-" It clicks. "Is it true? We actually won the war?"

"We won. We won, Sannie. But..." His expression softens. "They...You won't..."

And it dawns on her. That look, right there. San recognizes it. It's the same one her brother wore when he'd had to tell a ten year-old her father had been beaten to death in his cell.

San blanches. "Rose? Tae? Who is it? Tell me. They can't–"

She clutches the rim of the bottle–because she has to hold onto something: her whole world is about to crumble, and she along with it–and Leicester keeps speaking, telling her about Taeyang, and Saff, and Rose, who are dead.

"What about...What about Helio? He was their Secret Keeper. That means he's safe! I mean, what good would it do- what good–what–god, Lee, why are you looking at me like that?"

He just shakes his head, over and over. "I'm sorry."

As it turns out, the truth is worse than anything San could have imagined.

The weeks that follow are supposed to be the worst. They aren't, though. San feels mostly numb. Mostly. Something prickles the bottom of her conscience. She sits, perched on the windowsill, draped in velvet vulnerability. In her mind Helio cries, weeps, "How did you not know?"

I don't know.

San stays at home.

She's perched at the window, squinting to see the slivers of rain sobbing, slipping from her skin, spilling over her outstretched fingers.

You should have known.

The evening before, when he came back smiling that devious smile as he kissed her goodnight, he seemed so perfectly Helio. In the swirling evening, San remembers his hair, gloriously golden by the low lamp light, his eyes, and flickering flecks of the universe... He didn't look human.

The signs were there. He had not stopped moving for weeks, busy guarding his blank expression like a treasure despite all the horrors underneath. He had to have known his fate: that he would surrender to the Night.

The Night Helio died, he kissed her goodnight. His footsteps paused by the door. Beyond her room, everything was cold and dark. The kind of darkness that made monsters. He turned; San could only see half his face, but it was more than enough to watch the way his eyes stopped blinking, the way golden lashes froze against sallow skin until the pain passed. All she could think in that second was *I need him.*

It was a silly thought. He was already there.

Then he wasn't.

San is eighteen, and technically not allowed to drink. But here's the thing: civil unrest doesn't care about your legal drinking age. Isn't it sad? And if there's one thing the Scissors allow, it's drunkenness: it keeps the proletariat subdued.

Helio used to tell her not to drink, after he came home with hot sticky whiskey breath, but Helio isn't here anymore. San can do what she wants. She can't afford good alcohol–she can't even afford rubbing alcohol–so she steals it.

She ends up curled into a ball in the bathtub, acid gnawing at her insides until she pukes. When it's over, San straightens up and, against her better judgment, takes another swig. Her eyes find the skylight. She thinks she can see the stars.

Ridiculous. You can't find stars over the city; you can't even find the sky! It's all smoke, fog, smog...

It must have hurt, to die like that. Right, Helio?

Helio didn't mind the weather, but he preferred the sun: "That's what my name means, doesn't it?" She'd scoff. Sometimes she'd hit his shoulder and tell him off. Helio was named after a purple flower, not a yellow star.

He thought he was the sun god. He thought he'd live forever.

Oh, Helio. I told you, didn't I? You were mortal, just like the rest of us.

The drink fizzles in San's stomach. With a shiver, she hugs the bottle closer. In her dreams, Helio is everywhere. He's holding her by the waist, laughing; he's picking pieces of flour from her hair with that self-righteous smirk; he's kissing her forehead, telling her he's safe and she is too and he'll come back in the morning, he promises. He doesn't.

What was it all for?

She's awake. She stumbles by the light of the moon to the bedroom they shared. There! His bed. Sleepless nights, mumbled promises murmured into her hair, promises that are worthless now. San trails her fingers along the sheets, feels the rough fabric on the calluses of her hands. Then there's cracked cement; or her cracked soul.

It may be the alcohol fogging up her brain, but she thinks she catches a whiff of Helio's aftershave.

There is a small space in time made for you. You sleep there, you dance there, and you laugh there. You make it yours, yours alone, so no one can forget who you are, least of all you—that is, until you're gone. When you're gone, your entirety is erased in an hour; everything, but your initials scrawled on the side of a dusty urn. It's so tragic. Adults would sneer at her words, but it's true. If no one really matters, in the end, why is it so painful?

She'll be the only one to remember Helio, the only one to be constantly reminded that he is a traitor. She still loves him despite it.

Loved.

Loves?

Does love even have a tense? When the people you love die, does your love die with them?

No, she decides. If it did, it wouldn't hurt this much.

She'd like to hate him, she really would, but grief overpowers everything. She should leave now, she really should, but...

She has to learn how to sleep without him there, she really does, but...

The sheets look so soft, even though she knows they're not, and the pillow still smells like him. For tonight, she'd like to keep his ghost close.

There's no funeral. Helio is The Traitor. Even dead, the Opposition shows no mercy, just like the Scissors. They're all the same in the end, and apparently, San is one of them.

One of *them*. That's how she has been labeled. That's how the city works. Once someone close to you makes the news, you've been tainted—by extension. So if Helio is The Traitor, she is, too.

It's fine. She can handle the dirty glares and gaping stares, the crowds in the fog burning holes through the side of her head. She's had practice, hasn't she? After all, her father was The Traitor, too. It's the reason he was locked in that dingy cell and never came back to their dingy hell. He went to the *real* one.

At night San can't sleep, so she thinks. She hates it. She thinks about that time she and Helio made bread pudding in the kitchen after he came back from some ridiculous recon mission. She thinks about how she joined the Opposition straight out of school, and how she shouldn't have. But she did, because of Helio. He was so eager, too eager, to fight for what he thought was right.

It wasn't right. There was no right. All he should have focused on was *how to stay alive.*

It was stupid, maybe, but San realizes she was always prepared to die for him. She just never realized she'd have to live for him, instead. It's harder.

After her father died, Helio was the one who kept her company. "It'll get better," he said with that knowing glint in his bright eyes. "I promise. It *will* get better." At the time, he said it with such conviction that she actually believed him.

Yesterday, it was Leicester who told her the same thing. He told her it would get better. He told her, "Give it time."

Liar. What do you know?

That night, she dreams of sun-kissed skin and golden curls. She kisses him, wakes up, and hurls.

For a while, San keeps herself busy with the shop and, true to her resolve, never comes near his bed again.

Except once. It's too early to be awake and yet there she is.

"I miss you," she whispers to the dust. She's been saying it in her head for months, but this is the first time she dares utter it aloud. "I miss you."

The dust doesn't reply, obviously, so she moves away.

And freezes.

"Don't," the dust hisses; but when she turns back in a frenzy, there's no one there.

There never is.

5 Years Later

MIDORI MEHANDJIYSKY, 13

HADN'T REALIZED THAT IT HAD BEEN MORE THAN FIVE years since I've last been outside to smell the fresh air. All I've got is the smelly barrier of my hazmat helmet. Not once in five years have I held another person's hand, much less give or get a hug. Day after day, I sit in my room, or in the den if there is no one else there. But it's not just me. It's everyone in the world. We all sit in our homes, while the ptera-virus mutates each day, and there is absolutely no one to tell anyone that it's going to be ok, because it's not. No reassurance.

It was the middle of 2026 when it was decided that there would be no more trying to find a vaccine, medicine, or any kind of solution to help us battle the virus. It started mutating in around 2021. Back then, we thought the mutations would be manageable, but since then, there have been more and more mutations, the rate only increasing as time goes on. This is why, when it finally showed a consistent rate—mutation every month or so—we lost hope.

It's honestly crazy how the ptera-virus started from just a bat. A bat going about his daily life, not even realizing that he would be ruining everyone's lives forever.

It was difficult at first to get used to our new life, but soon we realized, when you get past the fact that if you catch the virus you are already dead, your biggest problem is boredom. Sure, I have online school, social media, and video games, but after five years of the same thing, you realize that even the things you love get tiring eventually.

In a situation like this, how does one make friends? There's no real answer to this question. At school, even if you decide to be brave and turn on your camera, you don't get to socialize with anyone really. I'm lucky that I still have a few friends from before this crisis even started, but it's almost as if we've all moved away from each other, since we can only communicate online.

Nowadays, I can't express my emotions anymore. I think that is the same for everyone. After being pretty much alone all of the time, we all now have a hard outer shell with many layers, and it's really difficult to get to the vulnerable bit. This is not only the case with emotions. After no real happenings besides an ongoing pandemic, you start to wonder, who are you really? There are no real components to your personality anymore.

I hung out with my best friend a few days ago, and though we can only see each other's eyes through the small window of the hazmat suit, which we have to wear if we are with another person, even if you are inside a building. It felt like a vacation and relief from the harsh reality that we live in. We talked together so familiarly, although everything around us has changed.

Recently, a study showed that people who suffer from depression are more likely to get the virus, and the virus worsens the depression. That's why I've been worrying about my brother. He's been very sad, lonely, and he's been avoiding talking to me and my family, even during dinner. Plus, he's been acting very strange lately. Our doctor told us to be really nice to him, and try to socialize, but even that he brushes off. I doubt that he has the virus, but I'm still worried.

My family and I were getting prepared to eat dinner. We each sat down, while unplugging each of our tubes from the food boxes attached to the wall. As we opened the valves in our hazmat suits to put the tubes inside our mouths, the phone suddenly rang. The air suddenly got chilly, but not just because of our air circulators. Honestly, it sounds like a scene from a horror movie.

It was just my aunt, so we were all relieved. But then, when she told us that my uncle, my mom's brother, had the virus, the relief vanished. My mother cried, and announced that she would try to visit him at my aunt's house. Of course, we tried to stop her, to tell her it's not safe, but she went anyway. To be honest, I don't really blame her. I would probably do the same.

After that, we didn't really finish eating dinner. We all went our separate ways, and when I was finally in my room, I got a video call request (the only way of conversation without a hazmat suit) from my brother. I immediately answered. He was clearly very scared; he was shaking. He told me that he couldn't believe that Uncle had gotten the virus. I nodded, adding that it's even worse that mom left to see him. Then he said, "Sis, I wish I could hug you." That melted my heart a little, if I'm being honest. I quietly said, "Me too."

We stayed on call for the rest of the night. Around midnight, we eventually fell asleep.

The next day at around noon, we got a phone call from my mom, who was temporarily staying at my aunt's house. She said that at the moment, our uncle was still alive, but he was having trouble breathing, and he kept getting an extremely high fever. She said that she might stay with our aunt for a while, and that we shouldn't worry about her. We all said our I love you's and then hung up.

School was boring again. I had a history exam. It was about the plague in 1665. But I don't see the point in learning the past, when you have no effect on your future.

I told my friends through text what happened. I received a lot of sympathy and hopes that they would be ok. Weirdly enough, my brother has been more social with me, and we've been calling pretty much every day. It's been really nice. It makes me feel a warm and happy feeling that I haven't felt in a long time. I really love him, and I know he loves me too. I can tell he's been making an effort to be more positive.

When we got the next phone call, it seemed almost impossible to stay positive anymore. The call was from my aunt again, telling us that our uncle had died, and that mom had an increasingly high fever. She sadly told us that she would try to take care of Mom the best she could, but she didn't think that she would be able to help very much.

This made dad cry quietly, my brother cry loudly, and me stare at the wall in utmost surprise, shock, and dismay. Why wasn't I crying? Is my pain and empathy gone? Why? I do care about my mom, I do. So what is wrong with me?

I sat down on the couch, slowly. My brother sat down on the other side of the couch, and watched me. "Are you okay?" is what he said to me. I didn't know the answer to this question.

"I..." was all I got out of my mouth. He nodded, slowly. "I understand", he whispered. He gave me a grim smile, and went to his room. Dad had already gone, so now it was just me in the room. I got up, walked to the bathroom, and looked in the mirror. My reflection and I both put our hands together. We stared at each other for a solid few seconds. We both had on our banana-colored hazmat suits on. Our brown eyes and hair were barely visible by the dark screens of our suits.

I went upstairs, sat in my room, and called my brother. We talked until Dad told us that dinner was ready. When we got downstairs to eat dinner, Dad told us that he wanted to talk. He said that he was sorry for not really saying anything when we got the call about Mom, and that we should all try to be positive, because you never know, there may be a chance that Mom will recover. This statement was what got me and my brother through the night. We were able to sleep with a smile.

The next morning, Dad told us that at around 3 A.M he got another call from our Aunt. She had cried, saying that mom started coughing up blood. She might not recover. He spoke to her as well, and she herself said that she was feeling terrible, and that she was sorry for putting herself at risk in the first place.

We were all glum for pretty much the entire day, and didn't really do much. Before bed I silently prayed for my mom to get better. *Please let her recover. Life wouldn't be the same without her. We need her. I need her. Please.*

When the doorbell rang at around 9 a.m., I answered it cautiously. My eyes widened, as tears flowed down my face. I could only say, "Mom...?" My brother and dad ran towards me. "She's here?" They stopped when they saw her. She had a small smile on her face, and she held out her arms. We ran towards her and had a big family hazmat hug. When all of that was over, we asked, "What happened? How did you recover?" She shook her head. "I wish I knew the answer. One minute, I felt like I was fading, but gradually, everything became clear. I felt stronger than I had ever felt. I got up out of bed, and I came straight home."

We were still gaping at her, and finally, my brother said, "Mom, that's ... amazing, wow." She nodded, but then her face turned grim. "We may have a possibility for a resolution now, but this isn't the end of our problems. After all, your uncle ..."

There was a small silence. Then, my dad nodded, and put his hand on her shoulder.

She managed a smile and said, "Well, I'm glad to be home!" She put her arms around my brother and I, and we walked inside together.

Though we still had many things to think about, it seemed like we were getting closer to happiness. It probably wasn't the end to our problems, but it did seem like a start.

Orbit

AIDA BROSHAR, 17

A PERSON SITS IN A CHAIR. A VENTILATION SYSTEM COVERS the lower half of their face, somewhat resembling an elephant in shape. Its tube coils down into a carved hole in the floor and disappears to an unknown origin.

Covering the floor is a scatter of knick knacks: forgotten notebooks filled with anything from class notes to half-written diary entries to sketches of machinery, a stuffed animal here and there, an old picture of a lake surrounded by green trees, a couple old helmets ranging from bicycle to astronaut, sheets of plastic and silicone, a pair of scissors, a half sandwich on paper.

Oddly, the only furniture is the one chair. It has a lever on the lower right that can recline the back.

The room is dark, save for the glowing screen the person is holding and the window that takes up one of the four walls. Outside the window torrent tornadoes of sandy wind. There's nothing but sand and wind beyond that window.

The person's screen clicks through different lessons as the hours pass. Sometimes it plays videos on history. *How did the 51st President save the U.S. from total destruction?* Sometimes science. *Here's a video of two kids your age who are absolutely LOVING this (extinct) plant experiment.* Other times math. *Here's how to do exponential functions to calculate stock value!* And finally: *You have 15 minutes to read and answer 15 questions to these utterly unprovoking passages, and no, we don't make exceptions.*

The person messily reads through the text and answers the questions. Occasionally, there's a question the person struggles to answer, hovering their hand over the screen between answer choices. It could be both, technically, but the phrasing of the question is infuriating.

A door opens behind the student in the chair. Light enters the room, though outside the door the lights aren't turned on except for some more distant. Someone enters the room. The newcomer is parental to the student in the chair.

"How is your breathing today? Air quality is terrible," the parent asks.

It becomes very noticeable the sounds of wheezing, patterns of stop-and-go in the breath. It feels like someone has wrapped a hard metal band around the student's lungs. When the student coughs, it sounds funnily like a bird.

"*Quack, quack.* Your best goose!" The student *quacks* again, this time it sounds like something dislodged itself in their chest. They lean forward to give their chest a nice *thud* with their fist but forget their hair is pinned to the chair by their lower back. Their shoulders move forward but their head snaps back.

"*Ow.*"

"Did you take your allergy medicine today?"

"Actually, yes. But I'm not allergic to smoke and sand particles, now am I?" The student waves their hand in emphasis. They toss their screen away from them.

"Don't throw that!" yells the parent. The screen hits the window. Neither crack. "Did you take your inhaler today?"

"Yes." A moment passes.

"You know–because of the smoke–I am always in a little pain. It feels like someone's taking a fork and twisting my insides. Like... like little bits of lightning, if that makes any sense."

There's a silence. The parent is visibly confused. They do not understand. Or maybe they do, but don't know how to respond.

"...But, I guess I'm lucky. Some other people are allergic to smoke.

"At least I have my breathing machine. Thank you government for at least allowing me that. Would be nice, you know, if you could deal with this" –the student tilts their head towards outside the window— "or not... which you all have been doing."

The parent stays silent. This isn't an unusual thing for them to do. They give no indication of their own beliefs, neither validating nor invalidating their child.

Inside the student burns a rage. Sometimes the rage is so hot it fills up their entire body to their eyes. Sometimes it's a cold, sleeping hatred in their fingertips. Other times it feels as though there is lightning in their scalp causing hair to fall out. It's aging. It feels disgusting. It feels completely inappropriate to be choked by these emotions, but perhaps the people to blame for these feelings are those who actually have power, yet can't seem to use it.

"How do you think they're doing up there? Enjoying the stars? Avoiding looking down at us? I know I would." The student gets up from the chair and walks over to the window. The air tube attached to their mask drags with them along the floor. They press their forehead against the glass, looking at the sky.

"They make it seem heroic—teaching us school from way up there." The parent is still silent. *We're in this together.* No, we're not. They just don't like feeling guilty and it keeps us complacent."

The parent speaks. "Where did you learn this? From school?"

"No. My friends. When we were able to talk to each other. And myself. Especially because I'm literally connected to a tube just so I can live and I know I'm not the people who caused high parts-per-million ratios in the air."

Silence, but not disapproving. "Well, I need to do work now." The student doesn't hear them. Closing the door behind them, it could be as if the parent had never been there.

The student continues to look outside, now watching the spirals of sand in the wind. They slide down the glass into a sitting position, still leaning their forehead against the window. It can't be a comfortable position. The air tube has reached its maximum length, pulling the student's face backward and down slightly.

Annoyed, they pull it off. An hour ago the air quality had caused a small asthma attack, making the machine pump medicine into the mask to be breathed in. They feel jittery, off balance, a little too light, and motor movement is only semi-reliable.

The screen lights up with a *bing!* It reads:

5th Consecutive Category 4 Hurricane Hits Southeast United States This Week: Which Sandwich Did The President Eat Today?

The student gets up, grabs the screen, and swipes past the announcement, only for an ad to pop up. It shows a nuclear family in traditional white American standard dress. They are laughing, surrounded by a version of island paradise, orbiting the earth.

Join us!

"Yes! Like that one animated robot movie–if I knew what that was," the student remarks.

They try to breath in. And find they cannot. The feeling of inhaling mud accumulates to small, sharp pains in the lower ribs. They spin around, disorientated, searching for their mask. There! They reach down to pick it up and almost fall over. At this point, the panic and leftover shakiness is making it a challenge of concentration to execute basic tasks. They manage to hook their fingertips on the lip of the mask on the second attempt, shove it onto their face, and then secure the straps around their head.

The light on the screen flares and a second ad pops up. It's a survey. The survey in question has four sets of pronouns listed but a user can only click one box. The student can't resist. They first click the pronoun box *she/her* but then pauses.

"No, you actually don't get to know anything about me. I don't exist" –the student unclicks her response and turns off the screen–"plus, it would be a huge violation of just me as a whole."

She lies on the floor. The way the mask is facing really makes it look like an elephant head.

A long moment. The sky is darkening. Though the sun was never clearly seen, it certainly is gone now. The student stays lying down even as the shadows crawl out, tendrils of light-absent choking the room.

"I don't know what to do!" She pounds her fists on the ground then jumps up. She paces diagonally in a carved out path amongst the floor clutter. It gives the longest distance before having to turn around (though the length of her breathing cord doesn't allow the full diagonal length of the room). Her shoulders hunch forward as she paces, her head tilted towards her feet. The imbalance of gravity causes a hurried, anxious walk– something that bodies the teeth-grinding, discontent feeling that only comes with having no meaningful control.

After a while, the person lies back down.

She would do something with her screen, but eye strain already is giving her a headache. She rolls over and grabs a mechanism from the corner and rolls back. It looks like a motorcycle helmet.

Taking off her breathing mask, she puts on the helmet. At the back, a hole shows a circular window of hair. Grabbing the mask, she twists it off and connects the tube to the back of the helmet so the air flows into it. What makes the helmet unique is that there is some sort of thin plastic where her neck meets the helmet edge. A sealing step.

The person puts her finger around the sealing edges, feeling for air leaks. None. A success. It would have been easier to simply keep the mask on, but wind storms are known for their blinding qualities. That's where a helmet with a glass front comes in.

She disconnects the air tube, reconnects it to the mask, takes off the helmet, and puts the mask back on. She bowls the helmet back to the room corner.

She kneels next to the hole in the floor where the tube emerges from.

She carefully inserts her hand, feeling for how she can disconnect whatever filters the air from the rest of the machinery. Theoretically, there should be some sort of device that is the home of operation. And, theoretically, it should be something easily handheld.

She'll need to carry it around, eventually.

The Aftermath

TEALIA JUD, 12

"**G**RADUATES OF 2096, IT HAS BEEN AN HONOR..."
            BOOOM

Mr. F Martin never finished his graduation speech because at that very moment the ground began to shake and alarms began to blare. Mr. F Martin fell to the ground. Mrs. Novel the headmistress of Yellowstone Academy of Science and Mathematics came on the intercom.

"Please quickly exit the area, please reach a safe distance of 100 miles from the school. This is not a drill, I repeat not a drill. If you do not do so you will most likely not survive the eruption of the Yellowstone Volcano."

Everyone looked around surprised but Grace was already on her feet and almost to her car. She had been the only one who had actually read the campus safety manual and she knew all about what to do if this happened. She had a motto taught to her when she was very young that you should always read the safety manual. So she had set up her car in case of an extreme emergency. She even had a secret compartment in her car that she used to store emergency supplies like oxygen masks, enough food and water to last for three years, duct tape, a first aid kit with a mobile x-ray machine and retractable stitcher arm to sew up cuts and, if you are really desperate, your torn clothes and several other necessary items. She opened her car door and said,

"Car drive to the west coast 90 miles per hour, initiate emergency car seal 2.46 Yellowstone"

The car shot out of the parking lot and began pelting down the road just as the other kids were rushing to their cars finally realizing what was happening. The ground was beginning to swell and steam was rising from the asphalt. And then when she was twenty miles away the ground erupted and smoke and ash billowed into the sky. She could feel the shaking of the earth below her as the car drove. She lay back hoping that she would make it.

As the car drove it played soft music. The car was big and she had installed some perks to her car such as a fridge, a foot bath, and the seats in the front had been replaced by a massage chair and in the back a small bed and a kitty palace. She looked over at Jasper, her Siamese cat. While she had lived at the university she had always slept in her car because cats or animals of any sort were prohibited and Jasper got lonely. Jasper stretched and walked over to her, she patted his head and opened a secret compartment on the floor and it was full of cat food. She took some out and put it on his eating mat next to his water dispenser.

"Lucky I just refilled your food compartment. You were down to only a few, this should last for at least two years."

Jasper meowed as if he understood that there was a problem that could not be solved by anyone. Grace looked out the back window and saw the eruption still happening but no one was following behind her.

"Car mileage update please."

A sweet female voice responded,

"We are a safe distance of one hundred and seven miles away from our starting point at Yellowstone Academy of Science and Mathematics.

"Thank you car that will be all."

Grace walked over to her bed and she pulled the drawer under her bed. She took out each of her supplies and counted how many there were. It turned out she had eight oxygen masks with one day worth of oxygen, eight cat oxygen masks with one day worth of air, her first aid kit that could treat minor injuries, three years' worth of nutri-bites which are like little candies that is like a feast packed into one, three years' worth of water, three rolls of duct tape, one oxygen tester, two changes of clothes and lots of other things to keep her and Jasper occupied.

She was satisfied with this stuff although now she thought about it there were several other things she would have brought. She changed out of her graduation gown and got into one of the changes of clothes. She put the gown in the drawer with the rest of her emergency supplies and then she closed it. She went up the front and sat down in her massage chair with Jasper on her lap.

"Car play the audio book Show Your Light by Gama Etemez, it's going to be a long drive" said Grace as she lay back in the massage chair and Jasper began to purr listening to the words of the book.

Finally about ten hours later the car arrived at the west coast. She knew it wasn't as far as the east coast from Yellowstone but there was no road from the school in that direction and she had wanted to get away as quickly as possible.

"So I guess this is where we are going to be for a long time, Jasper."

He meowed and closed his eyes again.

"Car, will the structural integrity of the car hold with the predicted amount of ash?"

"Yes, the predicted amount of ash is three-five meters and the reinforced steel, titanium and diamond should hold that amount." said the female voice.

"Thanks," said Grace as she walked over to the small bed. "Dim lights, keep temperature at sixty-five degrees Fahrenheit."

She spent the next months in her car with only her cat for companionship. Every day she turned on the radio and called out to the world and every day she was disappointed to find that no one answered. She constantly burst into tears at random times and wished that she had saved some of the other students at the Academy. She cursed the other students for being so dumb and not reading the manual for safety. But most of the time she sat in her massage chair staring at the outside contemplating leaving but she always told herself no mainly because Japer needed her.

Four weeks after she started her confinement she decided that staring at the sealing all day wasn't helping her stay the same so she turned to one of her passions. Grace had taken all of the stuff out of the drawer under her bed and filled it with the inflatable seed pods from her plant sciences class so that she could have fresh strawberries, tomatoes and of course catnip for Jasper. Every day she took them out and watered them one by one to make sure that each one got watered. She soon realized that they would need sunlight but the sky was black from ash so she left the drawer open and she hoped that the lights in the car were sufficient. About five months after she planted the plants all her hard work paid off and she picked the first strawberry off of the plant. About twenty-four months into her confinement in the car she looked out the window and for the first time in twenty-four months she saw that the sky was beginning to lighten.

"Car is it safe to go out there?"

"Yes, although you will want to wear a jacket it may be cold."

She put on a jacket and for the first time in two years she opened the door to her car. She stepped out onto the ground and nearly fell in deep ash. She looked around but here was no one in sight. She closed the door and instructed the car to do an oxygen clean so that the air would be clean of any tiny particles of ash. She stepped up on the roof and looked around. All she saw was ash, piles of ash everywhere, covering what probably used to be homes and towns. She feared there was no one except her left on the planet. She returned to the car.

"Car I want to use the sensors to find out if anyone is still alive out there and if there is take me there."

"It is very difficult to tell but if there was anyone the conditions are bad for sensors." said the female voice.

"Turn on the radio." said Grace. "If anyone is out there please respond, I must know if I am the last person on earth."

She did not really have any hope that someone would respond and she feared that the race of humans and all their accomplishments would die with her. She looked around at the car surrounded by piles of ash that had been her home for two years and waited for the response she knew was never going to come. Yet when she thought all hope had been lost a garbled static male voice came over the radio,

"Is anyone out there?"

Among the Stars

DORA GRAHAM, 17

"**S**TARS ARE ONLY PRETTY FROM FARAWAY"
The empty room didn't respond. The shining alabaster walls just sat, as they had for the last fifty rotations, in rigid standstill. The fact that the small craft was orbiting at nearly 690,000 km/h was hardly noticeable save for the slight shift in the viewport's vision of Earth's native star.

Quill was settled in the large circular window, studying the blazing horizon through shaded specs and penning in her journal.

"Their bulbous bodies are riddled with scars and pits."

She paused and looked back at the reinforced glass.

"It looks like my acne."

She jotted down one last note before leaning her head back and staring into the dark. Forty-seven days. If you could even call them that, what with night time existing as a constant all around her craft. Twenty days since evacuation, since she had seen the ground. Admittedly the cracked and swollen earth wouldn't be around for much longer, given the rate of solar radioactive decay, but still. She missed it. She never thought she would miss the dirt. Quill looked back down at her journal, the cover dog-eared and creased, and began to flip through the pages.

> Day 0001. Course bearing 060°. No change in solar radiation. Temp is stable.

> 0004. O2 filter is up and running. We are still on course. The air is different up here.

> 0011. Bearing 059° before correction. The sun is filling the horizon. It's stunning, I guess.

> 0021. The rattle in my lungs has almost faded. There are two-hundred and eighteen visible bolts in pod room C. Only two-hundred and thirteen in Pod B. I will recount.

> 0034. The rehydrated tuna wasn't as good on the second day.

> 0042. Still flying towards the sun. I thought I saw a cloud, but it was just a smudge on the viewport glass. Water vapor can't condense like that anyway...

As she continued flipping, a small scrap of paper fluttered out of the notebook and into the air. Something caught in her chest as the loopy handwriting registered. She plucked it out of the air and brought it in front of her glasses.

"mail me some space dust -X"

Quill stared at the note as her stomach sank. She blinked a few times and shook her head before stuffing the scrap back between the pages.

The dust had known her for as long as she could remember. It caked the walls of her bedroom, swathed up in clouds whenever she dared to venture outside. It lay in row after row of parched ground, nothing but dismal thimble weed managing to poke through. In the final months before her departure, it had started to coagulate in her lungs; she wouldn't have lasted long if she stayed. She was suffocating.

When she was young, Quill would stare into the night sky. She would wait for the glittering dark to enfold the planet in response to the retreating sun and would outstretch her earth-sodden palms to reach for the lights far above. Her mother had told her all about the fantastic adventures that were to be had in the outer rim. Filled with promise and prosperity and fulfillment, rocketing up among the stars was the dream of every child born onto the barren continent.

Now that she was up here, she couldn't complain, could she?

The cabin of the vessel had all the clean air she could ever need—it was recycled and filtered twice daily. She had enough packaged food to last her two lifetimes. Clean water. Not to mention the craft had a chess set. It was everything a teen could ever want.

She had reached for the stars and had made it. But even among a legion of glittering lights, she felt utterly alone, sequestered away in alabaster walls.

Turning away from the window, Quill launched herself further into the main cabin. Without the directional compass of gravity, she had to navigate her way by clambering across the space using intermittent handholds on the walls. Her hands shook ever so slightly between finding their grips.

How long had it been since she had sat in real moonlight? Even back home, it had been a long time since she ventured outside. The nights had only gotten shorter and shorter as the shadows waned with each passing rotation, and eventually the days just blurred together. And now she was floating in a hunk of metal in space where there were no days at all. She had escaped one endless cycle into the arms of another.

Once she reached the doorway, she turned back. The sun beamed through the port. Its light streamed in, filling every corner and every crevice; there was no shadow to be seen. The gleaming white walls were

almost blinding. Somehow, so much sunlight felt arti-
ficial. The whole room looked like something out of a
movie she was watching from afar.

All of the hiding and the preparation and the running and the launch—it had all happened so fast. She
barely had time to sleep, much less think while preparing, and now that she was here, all she had was time.
Her mind and body and lungs were all hers now, but
she had no idea what to do with them.

Quill let go of the wall and stared down at her hands.
They certainly didn't feel like her own. Her fingers moved,
but the limbs remained strangers. She had watched her
hands run calculation after calculation, adjust module
after module, and now they looked estranged being so
empty. For so long, all of her was preparation and anticipation and escape and now she was here. Holding onto
nothing, she drifted back into the room, spinning ever
so slightly as she relaxed her body.

How long had it been since she had seen clouds?
Those delicate puffs drifting aimlessly through the
wilting atmosphere. She had looked up at those too,
in all of their nonchalant detachment, and wanted to
be among them someday. Just floating. And now she
herself floated in aimless circles as the craft hurtled
through the barren void; layer upon layer of floating
in nothing.

The clouds had been so pretty from far away. When
she launched, she had passed up, up, and up through

them, dispersing the conglomerations of condensed vapor and soon they were nothing but faint white blemishes on a brown planet. An ache rose from the pit of Quill's stomach and lodged itself in her throat.

She wished she could go back to before. Before she passed through the clouds, before the clean air, before the sun was so oppressively close. Back to distant visions of lights and marshmallows in the sky, back to Earth and the dirt and the suffocation. Back home. She knew she couldn't go back, she would surely die. Now that she had seen the sun and burst the clouds, they would never, could never, be the same landmarks to her—they would float in a dying sky, distant and weightless.

And now here she was. Quill was the "good ending," the "hope of humanity," the survivor. One of mankind's dauntless pioneers, rotating with all the significance of every other system or body in the universe; just an abstract hope that could be dissipated or reduced with any amount of proximity.

But she was here. She shook herself, now rotating head over heels. If she was going to be on this ship until she reached new land, she didn't want to drift around anymore, just waiting. Stretching her neck side to side, she returned to the window and scooped up her journal.

Vermilion

MONIKA JOZIC, 13

VERMILION WAS HER FAVORITE COLOR. HAVEN ALWAYS FIX-ated on the objects tinted with that bright hue, no matter how scarce it was in the abandoned cities we found ourselves wandering through. As I watched her, she suddenly redirected her gaze from the non-functioning neon "OPEN" sign hanging in a broken window across the street. She adjusted her gas mask with a slight cough, signaling with a wave of her hand that we should head back to camp. I strolled up to her and helped fasten the mask straps.

"You think Esther started the fire yet?" I asked.

She glanced up at me and shook her head, a small smirk tugging at her lips. Esther wasn't exactly the most responsible member of our group. I shrugged on my backpack and began walking towards the crumbling building we were currently calling home. Inside, Esther was snoozing in a tattered cameo sleeping bag. A quick nudge with my foot was all it took for her to snap upright, eyes wide open. I waited a few seconds for her to assess her surroundings.

"C'mon we have to start the fire, it's already dusk and I don't want the walkers after us." I lit some dried hay and dropped it in a pile of branches, and the flames grew steadily. The glowing warmth lit up the scars that stretched down my arms and legs, sustained from climbing towers and trees to run from the infected. The virus had taken mere months to spread globally, turning even the most docile people into homicidal machines. Those who were lucky enough to avoid infection had to face the reality of their loved ones attempting to kill them in a haze of virus-induced rage.

As the heat enveloped me, I diverted my focus back to my companions. Esther seemed to be completely zoned out, staring blankly ahead. I playfully snapped my fingers in front of her face and before I could utter a word, I was on the ground with her hands around my neck. I flailed my arms, first trying to pry her off of me and then digging my nails into her thigh. Esther let out a cry and loosened her now shaky grasp, cowering away as quickly as she had sprung the attack. Her breathing was labored, and she held her hand over her chest as if to hold in her pounding heart.

"I-I'm so sorry, Karma, I–" she stuttered, gasping between words.

She backed away, falling to the ground and looking at her hands in disbelief. Haven started guiding her through the breathing exercises that we'd learned to do when she got like this. I touched my neck softly, groaning in pain.

"It's okay, it's not your fault," I sighed as I rolled into a seated position. Haven met my eyes and I smiled weakly, pulling one of our threadbare sheets over my body and attempting to find a comfortable spot to lay.

"Get ready for bed, we need to be up before sunrise tomorrow to head to the bastion in Westworth. I heard some people are gathering there, maybe you guys can make some friends."

What I didn't say was that I would be leaving them there. Through no fault of their own, Esther and Haven had made me stray from the search for my sister, who I had lost during the initial outbreak. I didn't know how much time had passed, but I knew I needed to find her or I'd lose the last of my human connections to this world. Mom and dad had already ... I stopped the thought before it took over.

The sound of Haven's wheezy cough was the closest thing we had to an alarm. I stood up, allowing the cold to nip at my skin. Similar to a freezing shower in the before times, it was the quickest way to wake up.

I grabbed the last few bottles of water and stuffed them into my backpack, then motioned for Haven to make sure Esther was awake. Just a few minutes later, we were jogging through the rubble that had been our neighborhood for the past week. We trudged through mud and gravel, clambering over broken down cars and concrete barricades until we reached a forest. The trees loomed over us, shade speckling the ground.

"Karma, how far away is the bastion?" Esther asked quietly.

She seemed to be avoiding eye contact with me since the incident last night. I looked at the torn map in my hands, channeling the cartography project I did in seventh grade history class to estimate the distance we had to travel.

"A few miles I think, we should get there in a couple of hours," I responded, folding up the map and sliding it into the pocket of my windbreaker.

Haven's face was flushed pink and sweaty. She sniffled and rubbed her eye with the back of her hand.

"You feeling okay, Haven?" I rubbed my hands together, a feeble attempt to warm them.

"I think I just have a cold, I'll be alright." She feigned a grin.

I could see through the facade. I smiled back, the expression not reaching my eyes. She pushed onward, cutting off the conversation there. The rest of the trek through the forest was cold and quiet.

Eventually, we reached a clearing where a large grey building stood. As we approached, we could hear some hushed chatter that fell away to silence. Inside the walls, there stood a small group of people with matted hair and mud-drenched clothing. They looked to be our age, young people prematurely thrown into adulthood by unfathomable circumstances. I reached up to touch my own tangled black locks, pulling a twig out of the knots.

"Hello...we are not dangerous," I sputtered at the strangers, with my hands raised to show that I was holding no weapons.

There was no reply. I glanced at my companions and nodded my head towards the back of the building. We moved past the group cautiously, claiming our spot by unpacking our food and starting a small fire. Haven slipped into another coughing fit, and at that moment I noticed several mottled red bruises dotting her chest.

"When did those happen?" I inquired.

We hadn't known each other for long, but I definitely would've noticed something like that. They had to be new. She traced the marks with a finger and then folded her hands in her lap.

"Oh...uh, I just got thwacked by some branches on the way here, I think!"

She bit her lip, looking unsure. I furrowed my brows but didn't push the subject. Esther reached for the small can of soup that I had just heated and took a sip, passing it to Haven next. Maybe not the best idea to drink from the same can with a contagious virus going around, but it's not like we had a better option. I raised my eyes to look at the other group and found them already looking at us. One of them flitted their gaze towards Haven before locking eyes with me. It felt like a warning. I tried to shrug off that feeling. They didn't know us, but they were just as paranoid. It was the one common characteristic that all uninfected humans shared, likely one of the reasons for our continued survival.

I turned back towards the fire. Haven was resting her head on Esther's shoulder, both exhausted after a long day of travel. It was rare to observe the kind of peace that rested on their faces. Esther met my stare, her expression softening further. I hoped that meant she knew I had forgiven her for the outburst.

Esther woke up first, an unusual but welcome occurrence, and started a fire to warm our side of the bastion. Haven was still fast asleep, which was also unusual. I looked around the building, but the other group was nowhere to be found. All that was left of them were a few pieces of paper and an overturned bowl. I took the bowl and left the paper on the floor, scanning the area for any other remnants of past company. All I found was more paper, shards of a broken mirror, and a piece of cloth. I caught a glimpse of myself, realizing for the first time just how gaunt I had become since being forced to leave home. I wondered what my sister would look like when we finally reunited. She was always so beautiful.

"Find anything interesting?" I heard Esther call out, dragging me back to reality.

"Nope," I responded. I headed back to the fire, where Esther was scribbling on a piece of paper. Haven was still wrapped up in her sleeping bag.

"Well, Haven's dead asleep," I chuckled.

Esther looked up from her drawing and shrugged. I stood up and began to pace around, thinking about where to go next. I had to find my sister. Was she even still alive? Before I could finish that thought, a blood-curdling scream pierced the morning air.

I rushed over to Esther, who was pointing at Haven with a shaky finger and warped expression, silent tears streaming down her cheeks. The sleeping bag had fallen open to show Haven lying completely still. Her body looked awkward, with limbs positioned at odd angles. I turned her over and saw that the bruising on her chest had spread to her neck and arms.

Vermilion blood dripped from between her cracked lips. A cough filled the silence, rattling out of her lungs. Haven lurched forward, eyelids fluttering open to reveal milky white irises. She touched a finger to her mouth, looking down at the sanguineous liquid with a twisted smile stretched across her face. Esther and I looked on in horror, frozen in place. Haven snapped her neck to look at us, a familiar rage building behind her eyes. We turned to run.

PerfectMatch.gov

CAMILLE S. CAMPBELL, 16

NAME: Odessa_G243
AGE: 18
DNA: Ideal Genotype
STATUS: Not sterilized
FOLLOWERS: 900,000
JOB: College student
RELATIONSHIP UPDATE: Engaged.

I now have a fiancé, according to PerfectMatch.gov. The notification buzzes on my phone, in the sound of wedding bells, as the government congratulates me on the selection of their *perfect* choice. Dread pours over me, as I skim the text, vaguely noticing that the engagement already has a few hundred likes on my social media page. Of course—my followers know who the *love of my life* is before I do.

I swipe right, and his profile picture projects in front of me, lighting up my penthouse. Anthony_F124 stands alarmingly straight, grinning so widely that his veneered teeth are almost painful to look at, even though they're filtered through a phone screen. He looks more like a cartoon than a person, with his empty crayon-blue eyes and photo shopped superhero good looks. Everything about him screams *fake.*

It doesn't matter, of course. What matters is what you show *online*–and your DNA, obviously. If the plague doesn't kill us early, Anthony_124 and I will marry within a few years and spend at least eighty happy years together, posting the selfies and assuring the government that we're happy as can be. This is how the government works. They engage you before you have a chance to find love for yourself. I knew that I'd be engaged eventually, but so soon.

The government won't force this life on me, I try to tell myself.

But it already has.

I gaze around my room. It feels like I'm living in a stranger's apartment, because nothing about this place is *chosen* or *different* from any other elite's living quarters. Each elite's 3,000 square foot apartment is scientifically perfect, with a slew of gadgets, a neon yellow hazmat suit, a disinfecting closet filled with UV lights to put a hazmat suit in every day and a green screen wall for fake social media vacation posts. Most of the walls are chalk white and covered with screens— some flashing with the government's messages, others displaying product advertisements. My walls are a million tabs that I can't close. Even as I sleep, the sound of the government's voice beats into my mind, until I can't hear my own thoughts.

I'm nauseous, and it's not just because of the bitter stench of antiseptics sprayed throughout the apartment. I *love* someone. And that person *is not* Anthony_F124. I grit my teeth, blood rushing to my head. Sweat slithers down my back, as I imagine spending the rest of my life with a *stranger.*

No.

My phone senses my grip tightening and my pulse kicking up. In his flat robotic voice, Mark (the all-listening Assistant) asks, *"Are you okay, Odessa?"*

No, no, I'm not.

"Perfectly fine," I manage.

"Playing Cold Feet App," he responds.

"I *said* I'm perfectly fine!" I blurt, but, alas! The blast of propaganda explodes from the phone.

Cold Feet, the app for all doubtful newlyweds, hosted by the President himself, or, more importantly, the most followed man on social media.

"Arranged married creates a society with no mistakes, no overpopulation, no sadness, no lover quarrels.... just perfection. There was a time when people would die of loneliness, shooting themselves up or coming sick and having no one to die with. The pandemic is as deadly as loneliness or being married to someone who will make

you miserable. Divorce rates climbed as choices increased. Choices breed unhappiness. There is only one person out there who is right for you: and we found The One. Because we know who...

I toss the phone on the floor and the audio cuts off, at least for a few minutes before it restarts. These phones are practically indestructible, but, for now, I can enjoy the rare silence.

Now, I can actually hear *myself* think.

When will they realize that love is more complex than a genotype, predispositions and personality tests? It's more real than Science, because there's no *fact* to it. It just *happens*. I'm one of the lucky ones, because I found *real* love and nothing will stop me from keeping it. Not even the government.

NAME: Jared_R474
AGE: 18
DNA: Non-ideal genotype
STATUS: To-be-Sterilized
FOLLOWERS: n/a, no social media
JOB: sanitization
RELATIONSHIP UPDATE: To-be-decided.

Spritz. Rub. Squeeze.

There's a rhythm to scrubbing the airport floors. *Spritz, Rub, Squeeze.* I watch travelers shuffle by, a sea of gray hazmat suits, identical to mine. Occasionally, a yellow hazmat suit wearer strides by, traveling first class, of course. Sometimes, I get so caught up in the work that I forget how much I hate this world—maybe that's the reason why yellows force grays like me to do back-breaking work.

So we never actually think about it all.

My DNA ended my life before it could begin. No matter what dreams I have, no matter who I aspire to be, no matter how hard I work to achieve something, I will always be a gray.

My burner phone buzzes in my pocket. It can only be one person. *Odessa_G243.* I'm glad the plastic mask hides my blush, as the robot slides by. Its cold eye sensors flash beneath its metal armor, as its software determines if I'm doing my job right. I dutifully mop the checkered gray floor, knowing that if I look at it too long, the system will register it as unproductivity—or worse, disrespect to the establishment.

When it rolls by to scan the next sanitation employee, I slide out the burner phone and check the text from Odessa_G243, the only elite who hasn't treated me like nothing. Maybe it's 'cause she's a dreamer, thinkzzing that divisions can be broken. I'm fooling myself when I'm with her, pretending that we have choices endless like the stars in the night sky. Hidden away in the secret rooms in the Dark Web, it almost feels like we're the only two people in the world. I replay those times in my mind, as I scrub the floors, awaiting the next stolen moment.

New Message—To self-delete in 40 seconds
From Odessa_G243: Meet me tonight, will send web address. I love you.
Love.

Not the insignificant abbreviated *ily* that everyone posts on social media. *Love.* I reread the message several times, trying to imprint the memory of someone *loving* me before the message disappears.

Odessa_G243

I change all my servers to private, checking the encryption of data to ensure that the government won't see where I'm going.
The dark web.
I slide on my headset and the green screens in my room turn into flashing pieces of neon and black code.

I squint my eyes, as the code distorts and curls around me, engulfing me like tidal waves. Thousands of web links pop up on the screens of my room and flicker like pieces of a moving puzzle. It's like being in a cave with a million fire flies—you're not sure which to chase. I pull out the keyboard and type in the onion web address, send the invite and hold my breath, watching as the entire room goes still like a frozen computer. *Please accept. Please accept. Please*

A hologram flashes before me, the data loading in chunks. A gray suit appears first, then a head of wind-blown shortcut black hair, since he probably just pulled off his hazmat suit's respirator mask. Finally, Jared's face sharpens in resolution, until it almost feels like he's standing before me, close enough to reach out and hold. God, do I want to pull him close and feel the warmth of *someone*. Not just a cold screen.

"Love, huh?" he asks, his mouth curving into a half smile. "Or is that just a ploy to get me here on time?"

When I don't return his smile or utter back a sarcastic comment as usual, his expression softens. It looks like he's going to step forward and reach for the illusion of my hand. Instead, he folds his arms and looks over my shoulder, like he's nothing more than a picture online that I'm just dumbly staring at.

"You're not supposed to love *me*," he mutters under his breath, looking at the status update that hovers above my hologram. The engagement status is displayed for all to see that I'm perfectly matched. "What's the point of bringing me here? To see your status update? *Fiancé* to the grand Anthony_F124. It's too late—"

"It isn't!" I blurt, wishing he would look me in the eyes.

"You're right," he whispers, "Because there never *was* a chance. What do you want to do? Run away?"— he laughs at the absurdity of it all—"Throw away *everything?* You don't want to live my life. No *love* is worth it."

"Ours is," I say, my voice raw.

"For whatever it's worth, I love you. Now, I'll say it again! Marry him!"

I can't help but roll my eyes, "Of course, because obviously I want to spend the rest of my life with someone who's more like a wax figure than a human."

"Come on, you'll get used to him."

"Not when I know you're out there," I shoot back.

"Why do you have to be so damn romantic?" he retorts, throwing his hands in the air.

I shrug my shoulders, "Because, you're a sucker for that kind of thing."

He shakes his head, exasperated, finally surrendering. "How *would* we even run away? Did you read about the steps in your romance guidebook?"

I smile victoriously, "Where are you right now?"

"A back-screen room in the airport. Why?"

"You have keys to every part of the place, don't you? Inside access?"

"Oh, no—"

"Think about it. You can make fake tickets, fake names, hazmat suits disguise our faces. We could fly out of this forsaken place and start new lives."

He's silent for the longest time. *Say something.* I wonder if the connection froze, until he leans forward and kisses me. Both of our holograms collide into each other, fusing us together. It's a tasteless, cold kiss, almost like kissing a screen, yet there's force to it, a magnetic force. As I lean forward, kissing him back, his lips press against mine, harder, giving away a positive and equal reaction. This kiss is false—and yet it feels so real. It's a promise.

When he pulls away, Jared's wearing the smile that tells me he's up to something, "I know how we can leave."

Jared_R474

This is the last time I'm going to see this airport. Hear the screech of the luggage machine, feel the antiseptics burn through my plastic gloves and constantly be reminded of the divisions of this world. Goosebumps run up my arm and something flutters inside of me. *Hope.* The foreign emotion both unsettles me and invigorates me, as I scan the flood of gray suits that go by. I want to rip off my suit and scream from the top of my lungs, *"I'm going to be free!"*

False tickets. Check.

Forged passports. Check.

Odessa?

Doubt slithers through me, as I watch the airplanes dart into the gray clouds. Ours will leave next. Forty minutes to be exact.

The voice sends a chill down my spine. Did I do something wrong? Was she held up? Arrested? Was the government listening all along, waiting for the chance to catch her—

Or maybe she's finally realized what a terrible mistake this all was.

Odessa_G243

I stand by the entrance of the airport, my limbs frozen, like unmovable blocks. I'm painfully aware of how the elites in yellow suits circle around the gray suits—they don't want to get close. This is Jared's life.

This could be mine—or worse, if they find out what I'm planning to do, they could imprison or even kill *me. What* do *they do with people who disobey the Order?*

The life I built here—all gone, traded in for a life on the run. I squeeze my eyes shut, picturing the city that I'm leaving behind. I imagine the iron and glass skyscrapers that are immeasurably high, like the odds stacked against us. My mind bursts with visions of advertisements flashing in shades of bright neon and lights reflecting onto the pavement. The shadows that they cast go unnoticed. Now, I see it—*this* is the division of the world. There are the bland gray buildings shooting from the ground, all so similar that you don't see them anymore. Then there are the colors that wash over blank streets, making this world so supposedly perfect. Yellows are the *color* in the world, the ones who rule, who are to be admired.

The lack of color is everything else, everything imperfect, the *gray* suits. A slice of rebellion cuts through me. No.

My life will not be dictated by someone else. I am not a yellow and he is not a gray. I am Odessa; he is Jared; and we are in love. I open my eyes and make a vow to myself: *you will never return here.* Without hesitation, I tear open the airport doors and make my way to boarding. All my doubt is gone; it's time to take matters into my own hands. I will no longer blindly follow the rules of the society.

I recognize Jared in the crowd, as he anxiously waits, his body tensed. I run up to him and take his hand. Even behind the hazmat suit, I can see his eyes sparkle with something that other young people will never experience: *love*. Feeling his hand in mine, I'm ready to take that step forward and never look back. When you're unapologetically in love, something changes inside of you. All of a sudden, sacrifices, risks, fears—they don't seem so big compared to what you have to gain. True love makes you stronger; it shapes you into the person you were meant to be, not what society tried to carve of you.

"Are you sure that this is what you want? To give up everything?" Jared asks me, his voice riddled with both hope and fear.

"No," I start, and, as his eyes fill with defeat, I continue, "No, I'm not giving up *everything*. I'm trading it for something better, for our life of freedom, of unknowns, for our imperfect beautiful life."

The Pied Piper:
A Dystopian Fairy Tale

CANA SEVERSON, 15

ONCE UPON A TIME THAT HAS NOT YET COME, THERE WAS A large country full of people. It was a rich nation because most of its earth was fertile, and they could grow food in abundance. But gradually, around the outskirts of the country, the ground began to die. The farmers and townsmen began to move inland, gravitating toward Tellus, the capital city. As more of the land died and more rivers dried up, more people came to the great city, relying on its seemingly endless resources. But then the city too began to fail. Its electricity went first, leaving the streets dark and the machines dead. Then food began to run short. Then water. Just when it looked as though the city itself would collapse and everything would be lost, a creature appeared in the distance.

It wasn't like any creature that land had ever seen. It was large, taller in fact than their buildings, towering over the wasted farmlands. And, as it came closer, they began to hear its noises. Every morning, it gave a shrill but hollow whistle, like the sound of breathing over the lid of a jug. For that reason, they began to call it the Piper. It came nearer, and the city sent people to meet it.

"It's huge," they reported back. "Made of something like metal, and in a cylinder-shape, but a little narrower at the bottom. It has different colored panels that all shifted and spiraled, like a metal tornado, but it's very alive. And..." the messengers paused, letting the people wait for their news. "It gave us food, or something like it."

The next day, more people, almost half the city, went out to the Piper. They reported the same thing: it gave its whistle then dispensed sweet tasting thin items, enough for all the people who came to it. A few went back to the city to report for the people who were still there, but most had stayed out by the Piper, ready for its whistle the next morning. Before long, the entire city had moved near the Piper, pitching tents around its giant metallic shape, ready for its gifts. The Piper still moved every day, but soon it was moving away from Tellus rather than towards it. Nonetheless, the people followed. And they continued to follow it, camping by it and moving with it, for years and years. Their nomadic life became regular as people grouped themselves into communities and even a government system that organized the distribution of the Piper's gifts. It kept giving, though no one knew its source, and it kept moving farther and farther away from the land they knew. But it didn't matter: it fed them and they were willing to stay with it. Before long, Tellus was a ruin, and there wasn't a person within a hundred miles of it.

Over the years, the Piper led them across the land, through forests and fields, even across a desert and a canyon.

"But I don't think I've ever seen anything like those before," Erit said, pointing to the misty shapes rising in the distance. She turned to her friend, Rama, who was walking beside her. "What are they?"

"I don't know. I've never seen them before, either."

"I think they're mountains," Rama's mother said. "I used to see pictures of them all the time before Tellus fell. But I think they're dangerous. I heard a story of some people crashing into one in a helicopter."

"Helo-copter?" Erit asked. "What's that?"

"Oh, they were great machines that could fly by spinning the blades that were attached to the top." The older woman sighed. "I wish you could remember things like that."

Rama's parents were always talking about how they wished their children could remember the old world. They told Rama and Erit stories of things they used to have, but neither girl could remember Tellus. They had been too young when the Piper came.

"Well, we've seen lots of things," Erit said. "We've traveled everywhere."

"But you've never seen what comes from staying in one place," Rama's mother rued. "Like books, and we used to have screens that ran off electricity and had pictures moving across them. And people used to live longer, 'til they were one-hundred sometimes. Now all this moving around is wearing on people. They're not living past forty-five now!"

Erit looked around her at all the wanderers, all of them walking towards where the Piper had moved. Everyone had stories of the old world and of things they had left behind in the city. Personally, Erit liked the stories, but she knew Rama didn't care much about them.

"What's it matter what was in Tellus?" she would say. "We're not going back."

Suddenly, the long, low note of the Piper sounded through the air.

"Oh, that sound is beautiful," Rama's mother sighed.

"Music," Rama agreed.

They began to set their camp for the day, and it wasn't long before one of the distributors came around with that day's meal. While they were eating, Erit looked up at the mountains again. Rama's mother had said they were dangerous, but they looked very nice to her.

It was a little less than a month later when they were right at the foot of them.

"They're huge," Rama said, gazing up at the peaks, which were lost in the clouds.

"They're even bigger than he is," Erit said, looking at the Piper, which was dwarfed by the mountains. And he didn't seem to like them very much. The creature didn't have a face, so no one could tell what it was thinking or feeling. People had tried to study it when it first appeared, but then it was decided that it wasn't worth the risk of damaging or angering the Piper. They needed its gifts too much.

But every so often, when the Piper moved from a place particularly fast or when it gave less than usual, people thought it was agitated. That day, the Piper never stopped moving so as to pass the mountain quickly.

The people couldn't keep up with it so they camped at the base of the mountains for the night. When it was almost midnight and the sky was completely dark, Erit thought she heard a noise coming from the mountains beside her. She wouldn't have paid attention, except it was a sound she had never heard before. At first she couldn't make it out completely, but when she got up and left her tent to move closer to the mountain, the sound became louder and louder. It was intoxicating, beautiful and melodious.

"It's music," she realized. Real music, strong, and sweet, a dance of tones and notes, the most beautiful thing she had ever heard.

She stayed up all night, sitting at the Mountain's base, and listening to the sound.

The next morning when the Piper sounded its call once again, Erit flinched at the sound.

95

"It's hideous," she said.

Rama looked at her incredulously. "No, it's not."

"It is. It's absolutely terrible compared to the Mountain's sounds."

"The mountain doesn't make sounds," Rama said.

"It did last night," Erit said. "Come closer to it. I'm sure you'll hear it."

"But we'll be breaking camp soon."

"Oh, come on. We'll be fast," and she took her friend through the camps and over to where she had sat the night before. "Just be quiet and listen," Erit said, closing her eyes with anticipation.

Sure enough, after focusing for a minute, she could hear the music again, the same cool, sweet melody as before.

"Isn't it beautiful?" she said, opening her eyes and smiling at Rama.

Her friend was quiet for a minute, but then she frowned. "I don't like it."

"How can you not like it?"

"I just don't like it," Rama shrugged. "It's too complex. It's too hard, and I don't like it."

"It's beautiful," Erit said. "It's the most beautiful thing I've ever heard."

"Well, I said I didn't like it. Let's just go back to camp." She turned around and started walking back, but Erit stayed a little longer to listen to the Mountain.

Several days later, the Piper had moved many miles away from the mountain, and it was starting to fade a little behind them. In front of them, a great plain was becoming clearer in the distance. They could see it as it sparkled and shone, and when the sun went down it looked like it was burning.

"Mother said she thinks it's a sea," Rama said. "It's like a lake but much much bigger."

"Hm," Erit said, but she wasn't really listening. She was looking over her shoulder at the mountain.

"Are you alright?" Her friend asked. "You've been awfully quiet lately."

"Yeah, I'm alright," she said, turning away from the peaks. "What were you saying? A sea?"

"Yeah," Rama said. "It's supposed to be huge."

"Can we go around it?"

"I don't think so."

Erit frowned. "Why would the Piper lead us to it? We can't go through it. It's all water, and we don't have any of those, what did your mother say they were called? Those things they had in the old world?"

"Oh, boats?"

"Yeah. We can't go over water."

Rama shrugged. "Oh, well."

"It's strange," Erit said, looking back over her shoulder again.

She thought for several days, considering the sounds of the mountain, and the Piper's new direction, and how she always flinched now when she heard the Piper's call. After hearing the beauty of the Mountain, she knew it was horrible. She didn't eat any of the Piper's gifts either. They no longer tasted sweet.

Finally, when the mountain was almost gone from sight completely, and the sea was coming clearer, she made her decision.

"I'm going back," she told Rama. "I'm going back to the Mountain."

"You can't do that!" Rama said. "You'll starve. You can't survive without the Piper."

"Yes, I can. Don't you see?" Erit explained all the things she had realized since the music of the Mountain. "The Piper isn't actually good."

"Don't say that! It saved us."

"But it doesn't give us anything real. The food isn't real, good food. That's why people don't live long anymore. It isn't helping us. And the sound, it's not real. It's not music. I know that now because I've heard the sound of the Mountain. That was real, and beautiful, and good. The Piper's call is hideous."

"Stop saying this stuff!" Rama demanded. "The Piper's not bad, and you're not leaving."

"Yes, I am. I'm going tonight, and I want you to come, too," Erit said.

"You're crazy!"

"Please, Rama. Come with me. Stop following the Piper. It's not helping you. It's leading us to nowhere. It's taking us to the sea."

"It takes care of us!"

"It keeps us trapped," Erit said, begging Rama to understand her. "It's not good, and it's not real! Nothing the Piper gives is beautiful."

"You're crazy!" Rama shouted again.

"Please, Rama!"

"I'm not leaving. If you really are, then good-bye, Erit," and she turned away.

That night, Erit started back for the mountain. It took her several days to get there, but she never thirsted or hungered, because the music got stronger as she returned. When she reached the base and started to climb, the music grew stronger still. Once she was at a high point, she looked down across the lands beneath her. Far away, she could see the people of Tellus, and the tall shape of the Piper as it led them to the sea. All at once, the huge creature went in, continuing deeper and deeper until the waves swallowed it. Erit turned away as the people began to follow.

She started to climb again, following the sweet strands of music until she was at the very top, where she reached something truly good, far greater than the fate of the Piper, and lived joyfully ever after.

The Train

ALFREDO ROMAN JORDAN, 16

THE DARK WALK FROM HER DAILY TUTORING LESSON TO THE nearest *MagneTrain* station was one she was used to. The feeling of fear was all too familiar to her, as she raced to the station, fearing that someone might jump at her from a dark alley. She could at least count on the comfort of knowing all the houseless and beggars along her route, and she was almost certain that if something was to happen to her, she would have them to protect her.

Tonight, was a rainy night, the neon lights reflecting on the wet and dirty sidewalks, keeping the beggars awake as they struggled to find warmth next to the heat ducts of various buildings.

The *MoodBoards* of various stores lit up. Some told her that she looked sad and needed a new shirt to bring up her spirits, others that she was visibly frustrated and needed a burger to relief her frustration, others told her that she appeared angry, and might need a baseball bat to let it all out. She knew the truth though, she wasn't just angry, frustrated or sad, and she was all those things.

As she approached the station to get the train home she had the same debate she had every day, to jump or not to jump. She had never done it, but she was set that today was going to be the day in which she finally let it go. As the information screen showed less and less minutes until the arrival of the next train she was more and more set. But as the train rolled in she realized that she couldn't do it, she realized, as she had realized every day that she had at least something to live for: a whole future, made up of thousands of days, some of them she realized would be shitty, but she knew in one of them she'd get married to a beautiful woman, and in another one she'd get pregnant, and in another one she'd see her son graduate. All things to live for.

As the *MagneTrain* left the station, she started, as she had done every day, to overthink about what would be waiting home for her. Would her father be drunk once again? Had her mother left, like she had done many times before? Did her father hit her again? For the whole ride she didn't have a positive thought at all.

As she took the short stroll back home from the station her strides became shorter, as she started to try to delay the inevitable. As she grew tired of getting wet from the rain, and afraid of the night roamers she started to run, faster than what she felt she had ever ran before and before she knew it she was by the front door of her apartment building. As she walked up the concrete stairs lit up by the familiar light of fluorescent lights reflecting off the solid blue walls her heart started racing. And as she arrived at her blue, iron door plastered with the number 54C she frowned at the lack of noise coming from her apartment; no screams, no music, no life. And as the door opened she found out why, a big red eviction notice was displayed in the *HomeDisplay,* it described:

"We are sorry to inform you that due to 12 missed daily payments you are in breach of contract and have to leave apartment block 35BH in the next hour, failure to comply will result in calling of *MaxOps* to forcefully evict you."

Her parents left the house in ruins, objects were scattered across the ground, the fridge was opened, no sign of valuables was to be seen, and more importantly, her parents didn't leave any indication of their whereabouts. As she became more and more nervous, she noticed the intruder alarm ticking, she had to get out of there as soon as possible.

As she left the apartment block and headed to the *MagneTrain* station she shifted through her phone, trying to find a message from her parents, but there was nothing, not a single indication of their whereabouts. Now instead of shifting through her phone her mind shifted to her future.

What would she do? It was 11:32 p.m. *Where would I stay?*

The decision was obvious, she had to head to the group of houseless that she was familiar with. As she again boarded the *MagneTrain* back, she didn't even think about jumping, and as she got off the train her mind hadn't drifted a single bit. As she arrived to the dark alleyways she explained her situation, and the houseless offered an inflatable mattress and a baby blanket. That night wasn't rough at all, she instantly went to sleep, her mind tired of trying to find a solution.

As she woke up the next morning, she packed her few belongings up and left for school, where no one could know about her situation. In the city it was taboo to be abandoned, a sign of how low you had fallen in the social ladder. In class only one thing roamed her mind, how could she go from living a horrible life, to living an even more horrible life, why was life treating her this way.

That night she walked back to the dark, now wet and rat-infested alleyway, to rest and think about her next move. When she walked by the *MoodBoards* they didn't even light up, only saying that they couldn't detect a marketable emotion, and even more weirdly the *CyberWomen* didn't try to harass her to try "free samples" of products, instead just starring right at her with emotionless eyes. Her mind was cloudy, she didn't know if she missed her old life or if she was better off now, she didn't know if she should go to school or just beg for money, and most importantly she didn't even know what the purpose of her life was anymore.

As her feeling of self-worth started dropping, and the *MoodBoards* lit up with negative emotions, her feet carried her slowly to the *MagneeTrain* station, a simple routine that today would have a twist. As she arrived and realized there was only one minute left for the next train she didn't even flinch. She had stood there hundreds of days before, she had had the impulse hundreds of times, but this time every neuron in her mind was off, and only her heart was guiding her. As the train started rolling into the station she started walking towards the track, and as the train got slower her strides got wider. For every stride, the music of her heart got louder, each beat getting stronger and closer, like an orchestra about to finish their last song. As the soft violin tones ended, the drums started, the epic melody was about to end. Until, out of nowhere a *CyberWoman* snatched her back hand, and inserted a pamphlet into it. Delaying her for enough time that the melody would have more songs to play, and as the *MagneTrain* rolled away, her senses came back and the *CyberWoman* disappeared, just like a fallen angel.

As she left the station, she read the pamphlet, which read:

"Looking for line chefs – No experience needed – Good pay – Start immediately"

She thought about the offer and decided to call the number in the back of the pamphlet.

After a short interview she had the job. That night, the sun had dried up the wet ground, and she had her first good night's sleep since she could remember.

The next months were unimportant. She worked the whole summer, she went to school, and then she graduated. She was alone at her graduation, not a single clap for her in the audience. Life started to seem normal, until, one night, as she got ready to close the diner to the sound of soothing piano, the rain set in, the rats crept into the store and a taxi rolled up. In it was a faint figure.

The figure waited in the taxi for a solid minute, as if expecting someone to walk to her. As the figure grew inpatient, they went into the now dark diner and asserted:

"Look at what you have become. My daughter, working in a dirty diner."

"Oh, Mother, didn't expect to see you here, dressed up in such fancy clothes. Remind me, when was the last time I saw you," the girl replied, with a faint but threatening voice.

"Come on, don't remind me of how I left you, I always regretted it," said the figure in a sweet but malevolent tone.

"If you had always regretted it, why didn't you come back for me? Where you too busy climbing up the social ladder to remember your daughter?" Tears started to form under her eyes.

"Look, when your dad left me, I felt lost, so I found someone new, someone who could actually provide for us."

"Us? There was never 'us' in your imagination, you only cared about yourself and your rich husband. I have been doing great on my own, I have a job and I am going to start community college soon. I don't need you" She swept her tears and switched her voice to a threatening, uncomfortable tone.

"It's ok you think that, teenage girls like you tend to be dramatic, I am giving you an escape plan and you are not following it. I thought I taught you to take the best path at all times."

"Dramatic? You and father never realized, but walking back from school was always a challenge, I always felt like ending it because I knew, I knew that I would come to an unstable house, with an abusive father and a careless mother. Look mother, I am not saying that father leaving you is your fault, but me leaving you is. While living lavishly like you are doing might bring me material happiness, my mental health will suffer, and taking care of myself has started to be my top priority, maybe it should be yours too. So now, please get out of my diner," yelled the girl, with a feeling of empowerment and freedom.

The figure didn't flinch, instead she just left, without a single visible emotion. The girl felt a strange feeling of liberation, as if there wasn't any strings attached to her past, allowing her to focus on her future, and that she did.

As the months passed, she bought a small apartment, started taking community college lessons and more importantly started going to a therapist. She then met someone, a beautiful woman, and they eventually got married. Together they had a son, and she has never been happier. Today she told me why she finally saw true light when she saw her mother, she told me she didn't want to force herself into a negative loop again, and that even if she could have been happier with a lavish lifestyle, was it worth risking all the self-improvement she had worked on up to that point?

Dearest Seacat

JORDAN HINES, 16

T HE PORTHOLE IN THE SAILBOAT CABIN HAD A PERFECT VIEW of La Rinconada. As she looked through it, Lillian felt the strange sickness—of the sea, or for that sense of home she had almost forgotten. Yet, the boat never dared to creep closer. Once a major gold mine of Peru, this was now the last known civilization—the last that was high enough for solid ground—and the boat had been circling it aimlessly for days.

What was really sick were her cravings for the awful cuisine back on land. Like algae salad. She definitely could've gone for some algae salad.

On a ration day all those years ago, Lillian was twelve, and her stepmother had come home with slimy

Tupperware. She slapped it onto the table, waking the sleeping Lillian, who only rubbed her eyes and turned over. This was the best she could do once the hunger fatigue had settled in. "Get that out of my face, Nancy," Lillian said.

"It's algae for the foreseeable future. You're still gonna turn stuff down?" Nancy said. "Some people call that class," Lillian replied, uninterested.

"My dear Lillian, I call that entitlement," Nancy said. She went to the sink, and Lillian heard the bucket water pour over cracked hands. Then a sigh of frustration. "What's the problem, dear?" She looked over her shoulder and stared Lillian down with that wisdom she'd had since they met: the kind that seemed motherly and chest-beating all at once. It was strange, considering that their age gap only stretched a little past a decade. But maybe that was all it took in order to learn everything.

"You sound like you already know." Lillian didn't have another answer.

Nancy turned around and took a towel from the counter, tossing it between her hands to dry them. "I don't, actually. But Lillian, you're going to eat. Hand me my apron. It's going to be fine." She sprinkled the spirulina onto some old store-bought sugar cookies, and that was the last time they had something sweet.

It didn't take long for their house in Alma to flood. Then they were on a steady retreat into the Rockies, their whole lives stuffed into backpacks. The way their world ended was a slow, cruel race against time, and any existing government crumbled. No cautionary tales were made public when the water swelled over the beaches–around the time when Lillian was born–and no one told them what to do after their house had been submerged. Somehow, constant travel brought more isolation than either girl had ever experienced.

Being on the run could have been an adventure. But within a year, Lillian had grown enough to stop seeing it that way, not to mention her duty to the sick Nancy, now a slight mess of lumps and night sweats. She had slumped onto a boulder, wiping the drops on her forehead, and Lillian rushed to her side. The sea level was a good stretch of miles below them, so it would be worth the break. But the unpredictability–not knowing what she'd see if she ever looked down–still unsettled her.

"What is it?" Lillian asked. She looked at her stepmother, rubbed her shoulder, trying desperately to imitate that wisdom that had looked so reassuring not so long ago. "If we had a doctor, they'd tell you," Nancy said, laughing. "You're doing good. You're much stronger than me anyway."

"Yeah, you're doing good too, though," Lillian said modestly.

"For a dying woman, I'm sure." And the woman laughed again. "Here, I have something to show you." She reached into her bag, and pulled out a book that could fit in her palm. It was the kind that had been loved by a toddler all too well: yellowing pages, a delaminated cardboard spine, and a missing back cover. She read it to her; it was a hearty, swashbuckling tale of a cat that was associated with the sea, of all things. The Cat overcame her fear of water, and fulfilled her dream of sailing the open ocean. Leaving everything behind, she wanted for nothing. She was free. "The Cat thought that, well, everyone else could pound sand for all she cared," Nancy read.

Lillian glanced at the text again. "It doesn't say that."

Nancy sat up straighter, and once again, Lillian was proven to be the child. "But it does, doesn't it? What kinds of books do you think I would read to you when you could do it yourself?"

"Sorry, was that too entitled of me?" Lillian smirked.

It took Nancy a moment to process, but slowly, she understood. "Oh, you need to let go of things. What I simply meant was, we will survive this."

Against everything, it was the kind of book Nancy had left to her in her will, along with a kaleidoscope. Nancy used it as a fidget for as long as Lillian could remember. Lillian wasn't surprised, as one could only fit so much in a backpack; she wasn't upset either, as this vagueness was just like Nancy. The funeral was a small one, held in a little campsite they had been passing through. The officiant was a middle-aged man named Albert, who tried to comfort Lillian to the extent that a stranger ever could. He had lent her an extra tent, and she had set it up right in front of Nancy's final resting place: a mound of dirt, decorated with scattered pebbles in lieu of a gravestone. She stayed for weeks.

Nancy was a good stepmother. Not that Lillian had ever known her mom for long enough to play the comparison game; she died in childbirth. She couldn't remember anything remarkable about her father, but she supposed that was the result of not really being there. He had married

Nancy for the sake of appearances in the last year of his life, and then the young Nancy had found herself taking care of a girl in the middle of the apocalypse. And maybe that was better than anything that Lillian knew to ask for.

Albert broke the silence from outside of the tent one morning. "Take another look at that bedtime story. Forgive me, but I think...I saw something in it."

She wasn't close with him at all, so it's not like she could have been angry, even if she wanted to. But at this point, she had lost all of the fight in her. The loss was too great. "The inside of the cover. That's all I'll say," he said, and she heard him taking a few steps back. Lillian snapped out of it, realizing that she didn't really want to take another look at it; realizing that she hadn't ever done so on her own. But she replied by opening the book anyway, wanting to be strong. There was a note tucked away, etched into the dust jacket flap:

Dearest Lillian,

I was a person before I married your father, and a person afterwards. What's interesting is that I was a bit of a swindler. I'm not sure how, but that's how I pulled together this little surprise for you. Follow the map. Your hint: I have a feeling that your life will be inevitably buoyant soon.

I can't help you much with resources from where I am now, but I'll let you in on my secret: trade away whatever for something slightly more valuable. This is the way it boils down on the sea.

Don't trap yourself. But I have all the confidence that you will be okay. Thank you for being my Cat in the middle of this ocean. It's been an honor, dear.

"Are you okay?" Lillian looked up to see Albert peering in at her. She felt heavy. "Yeah. Thanks for this," she said. Lillian gave a final wipe across her hot face. She noticed a new color in the brush, and tried to distract him with it. "You know, I think Nancy's missing something."

"What's that?"

Lillian stood up, cracking thinned knees, and stiffly walked to a baby patch of pink flowers. She picked a few, letting her fingers be tickled by the white whiskers on the stems. "I didn't think anything this beautiful grew so high up."

"Those are red windflowers. An excellent choice," Albert said, before smiling sadly. "My daughter's favorite."

Lillian didn't pry—in fear of comforting sad people—but she said, "Then, this is for her, too." He seemed to cheer up as she placed them down on the mound.

"I think I'll be leaving tomorrow," she said. "Nancy's got a boat waiting for me." "Oh." Albert was still processing as she spoke again.

"Would you want to come with me?"

He hesitated, with a longing look in his eyes, for something that he didn't want to leave behind. "I think

I might be done running, but I'll think about it. Being a funeral officiant can get a bit depressing, to be honest."

Lillian had inspired him to refuse the grave, and he left with her the next morning. They followed the map a little ways down the mountain, and they found a little miracle of a sailboat bobbing on the water. The rope tying it to a tree was ridiculously long, and it was hard to guess how long the boat had been waiting for them. The neat script on the rear spelled a name loud and clear. The sailboat was named *Little Cat*.

Lillian finally collapsed at the sight of it, crying in earnest. Albert stood next to her quietly, his hands folded behind his back. This was always the feeling he knew all too well, and he had nothing but respect for such a strong woman.

They spent the next four years on the *Little Cat*, scavenging and trading for scraps. That was all they wanted, and they were free. But either way, La Rinconada was not accepting any more residents, and their resources were all but gone. They had squeezed all that they could out of Nancy's secret.

A call of her name came from the deck, and she tried her best to sit up straighter. Albert's head popped down from the stairs. "You alright, Captain?"

"I will be." Lillian said, trying to stifle a groan. She had become so hopelessly thin, even though she had sworn to Nancy that she would never let herself get to that point again. "Haven't we circled around this hole long enough?"

Albert stuttered for the right reaction. "I guess. I just know that I never want to have a floating remnant of ceviche ever again."

"We've become Mother Nature's bottom-feeders," Lillian laughed. He smiled. "Hand me her kaleidoscope, would you?" she asked. "It's a little far." Albert nodded and pushed the toy towards her, though with great difficulty. She felt bad as she watched his bony face resist a pained contortion.

Lillian picked up the kaleidoscope and rotated the cylinders, focusing her personal spyglass. The colors merged like stained glass, creating little mandalas for her eyes only. It clicked.

"I need some fresh air," she said.

"Sure thing."

They struggled up the stairs—clattering disasters of skin and bones—trying to help each other as best as they could. Lillian quite literally had to crawl across the deck, but finally, she reached the steering wheel. Albert settled against the mast.

"You want some privacy?' he asked.

"Yeah, maybe."

"Goodbye, then," he said.

Lillian waved weakly. "Goodbye," she said, and she shifted to lean against the other side of the wheel. She closed her eyes, and breathed.

"Isn't it everything you've ever wanted?" This voice was female.

Lillian opened her eyes, and Nancy was standing in front of her, red windflowers strewn in her hair. There seemed to be a glow around her, and she had never looked so alive. "I guess I'm so close to the end that I'm seeing you, huh?"

Nancy chuckled. "You look good, though."

"For a dying woman, I'm sure."

Nancy knelt down to Lillian's level, and they embraced with the struggle of survival, the wisdom, the hunger, everything...and this feeling of acceptance of that end. "I don't feel so sick anymore," Lillian said.

"I didn't either," Nancy said, patting Lillian's back.

"Do you think I led them well?"

Nancy pulled back to see tears on Lillian's cheeks. "Yes, and I'm proud of you. Look at who you saved." Lillian turned, and she saw that Albert was fading quickly. But he was fading into a hug with a young girl that resembled his spirit in every way, and he looked happier than Lillian had ever seen him. Nancy pulled a flower out of her hair and tucked it behind Lillian's ear. "This was all you, and it always has been."

Lillian nodded. "I'm happy to have you back."

"Did that work?" Nancy asked, pointing at the kaleidoscope in Lillian's palm. She lifted it to her eye for one last look, and what she saw matched this place. But she knew now that as long as she was there, everything would be fine. Even this—just a random coordinate in the middle of the ocean—could be her final resting place.

Have You Seen This Person?

NICHOLAS HULL, 12

MARGARET BURKE WOKE WITH A START. *WHAT WAS THAT noise?* She wasn't used to it.

"Wait a second, today's my first day of middle school! I forgot Mom set my alarm clock!" She rushed out of bed and put her best clothes on. She ran down the stairs. "Morning, Mom!" she yelled as she rushed past.

"Well, good morning to you too, honey. Just don't forget to eat your breakfast," her mom said.

"Oh yeah," she said, dumbfounded, "I completely forgot. I'm just so excited about school."

"I know you are, honey," her mom whispered, "Now go get 'em."

"Aye-aye, Captain Mom!" she said with a laugh, giving her mom a kiss before she grabbed her backpack.

Margaret sprinted out the door towards the bus stop. She was on her way to school.

"What's up, guys?" Margaret asked her friends as she sat down.

"Nothing much, I just got back from summer camp a few days ago," One of them said. "That's cool, Lily," Margaret replied, "What about you, Kate? How was your summer?" "Oh, same old, same old," Kate said, "I went to the library a lot and went swimming at the neighborhood pool."

"Nice," Maggie answered.

"Hey, you haven't told us what you did, Maggie!" Lily mentioned.

"Yeah, what did you do?" Kate added.

"Stuff I normally do," Margaret said, "I helped my mom with baking and gardening and whatnot. But that's not important right now. Let's talk about how middle school's going to be!" "I bet it's awesome!" Kate said excitedly.

"It's gonna be great!" Margaret answered.

Once she got to school, she knew she was right. She made new friends, caught up with old ones that she lived further away from, liked her teachers, and had so much fun at recess. On the ride home, she was thinking about how great it was. School was perfect, her house was perfect, and her life had been perfect for the past year. But soon after, the bus drove past a dark alleyway and she saw someone. Someone she knew.

"Dad?" she muttered under her breath as they drove past, "No. No, this isn't possible. How? Why? He's been dead for two years." She kept saying that to herself all the way home. She walked in the door and her mom immediately noticed something was wrong. "Maggie, what's wrong, sweetie?" she asked.

"Nothing, mom, just leave me alone," she snapped.

"No, Maggie, really. What's going on?" her mom said.

"Why does it matter to you?" she questioned.

"Maggie..." her mom answered, clearly irritated.

"Answer my question," Margaret said.

"Please tell me. I can make it better," she explained.

"Mom, just SHUT UP!!!! I'm not a little kid anymore! I am in middle school! Why do you need to know everything that's happening in my life?" Margaret yelled. She had never yelled at her mom like that before.

"That's it! Go to your room! You're grounded!" she replied. "Unless you drop your attitude and tell me what's going on."

"Nothing is going on, Mom! And anyway, I don't care about being grounded!" Margaret said.

But deep down inside, she really did care. Once she got to her room, she had a conversation to herself. She hadn't been grounded since before her dad died.

"Stupid mom," she said as she rubbed her hand slowly over her techno-bow.

"Stupid grounding," she then pulled back the metal-lined string as a heavy arrow was summoned in between the string and handle.

"Stupid life," she released it as it hit the target across the room with a thump.

"Stupid, stupid, stupid. If only I hadn't gone to school, maybe it would have spared me from this whole mess. Wait, that reminds me, I need to go talk to Dad! I need him to answer some very important questions. Like why he's been gone all this time. That's it! I'll run away and find him!"

That night, she gathered supplies. She decided she would bring her techno-bow, her sleeping bag, a compass, her phone, her hover board, fifty dollars, a canteen, and some food. Then she stuffed them all in her backpack. She was ready.

"Goodbye, mom," she whispered as she went out the door, "I'll see you when this is over." She then trekked off into the night. When she got far enough away, she fired up her hover board.

"Let's do this," she said with confidence, riding away into the air.

The next morning, Gail Burke woke to find her daughter missing. "Margaret?! Margaret!?!?!?!? Mmmaaarrrgggaaarrreeettt!?!?!?!?" she yelled. "No, no, no!! Where has she gone!?! MARGARET!!!"

Little did she know, her daughter was closer than she thought. She was only blocks away, looking in the dark alley for her father.

"This is where I saw him yesterday. He can't be far from here," she said, then she gasped, "Tracks! This is just the sort of clue I need to find him!"

Meanwhile, at her house, her mother was packing up supplies to go look for her lost daughter. She even made "lost girl" posters! "I need to find Maggie. Who knows what trouble she's getting in right now?" she said to herself. She then set off to find Margaret.

While her mom was busy packing, Margaret was at a store a couple miles away, asking around to see if anyone had seen her father, "It should be a few more hours and I'll have found him. Excuse me, sir, have you seen a man that looks like this anywhere around here?" she said, holding up a picture to the store clerk.

"Why, yes, I have," he answered, "He bought a pair of binoculars from me just a few hours ago."

"Thanks for your help, mister!" she yelled as she ran out of the store.

"Anytime, little girl. Anytime," he replied.

"Now I'm back on the trail," she said to herself, walking down the street, "he must be at the wilderness park. Dad loved bird watching. I don't have a map though. Plus my phone doesn't have Wi-Fi. Wait a minute, I have a compass! I know the wilderness park is in the northern part of town. I just need to go north!"

Coincidentally, Gail Burke was just a few blocks away and was trying her hardest to locate her lost daughter, "Hello? Has anyone seen a little girl who looks like this?" she yelled, pointing to a photo of Margaret, "Please? My daughter is missing, and I'd like to know if anyone has seen her!" It wasn't working, "I need to try a new approach. Wait a minute, I can track her phone! Why didn't I think of that before?"

So on that thought, she turned on her phone and started tracking Margaret's phone. It led her to the last place Margaret had cell phone reception, the store.

"Hello, good sir, have you seen a girl come in here that looks like this?" she asked the store clerk, holding up her picture.

"Yes, she came in here asking if I had seen a man in a picture and then she ran down the street towards the wilderness park," he said, "I hope this is of use to you." "Oh yes it is," she replied, "Thank you, my good man."

"It looks like I'm getting close," said Margaret as she was walking through the forest, "I should find him any minute now. I need to find the bird sanctuary."

But as soon as she said that. She bumped into a man. "Hey, watch where you're goo..." he stopped as she grabbed her techno-bow out her backpack and aimed it at him. Then he gasped, "Maggie?"

"Dad?" she questioned as she dropped the techno-bow, "What are you doing out here? Why haven't you been with your family? Did you fake your death? Did someone kidnap you? Why were you gone? WHY? WHY? WHY!"

"I-I-I got to go," he said.

"NO! You aren't going anywhere! Not until I get some answers!" She yelled as she tackled him to the ground.

Now she was crying.

"You've been gone for two years without us thinking twice about it, and I want to know why! You owe it to me! In the first year you were gone, you wouldn't believe the things I went through! I couldn't feel good enough to even talk to my best friends. So I lost them for a long time! You owe it to me."

"I will answer all of your questions if you let me go," he replied calmly, "It's good to have questions, just don't let them overflow. Now let me go, and I'll answer all of your questions."

"No," she said, "You're just going to try to run away again. You're staying here. Then a familiar voice jumped in, "Maggie?"

"Mom?" she said, running over to her, "Mom! How did you find me?"

"I tracked your phone and it led me here... Bill?" she asked, clearly surprised. "Um, hello, Gail," he replied.

"Why did you pretend to die and leave me with your child?" Gail screamed as she slapped him across the face with the back of her hand. "I've done all I could to help her! And what have you been doing, gambling?"

"Okay, fine," he said, "I will tell you why I left,"

"Finally," Margaret whispered.

"I had to cover up my tracks because I needed money and you refused to give it to me," he explained, "I had to steal to stay alive. You wouldn't give me the money I asked for. They wouldn't suspect me if I was supposed to be dead. Even though I covered up try tracks, they still got very close to finding out who I was. I barely made it past the police during that heist. I finally made enough money to live a steady life. I was going to return at some point but now it just feels like it's wrong and I should just leave you alone."

"That's all?" Margaret asked.

"Yes," he replied.

"Mom, why didn't you give him the money he asked for?" Margaret questioned.

"Well, um, because your father and I were growing apart, honey," she said.

"But can't you guys make up?" Magie asked.

"No. It can't be fixed. We fought many times and we wouldn't share. We wouldn't even look at each other at certain points. We were heading for a divorce. But then he left us. I came this close to depression and there is no way I am living with and loving that horrible man ever again! That's why we can't make up, honey. Now, come on, Maggie, let's go. " her mother said sternly.

"But what about dad?' she said.

"Let's leave this scoundrel alone," Gail replied, "Oh, and Bill,"

"Yes?" he replied.

"You were right about one thing," she explained, "you never should have come back. Everything was running like business as usual and then you stepped in and messed it all up." "I'm sorry," he said.

"Save it. I don't want to hear another word out of your mouth, you filthy rascal!" she answered.

But she didn't lead her away fast enough to stop Margaret from giving Bill something. He opened his hand. It was the fifty dollars she'd taken on the trip.

"Bless you, Margaret," he said.

"You're welcome, Dad," she told him, "You are and always will be, the only real dad I'll ever have."

"And uh, that's the whole story. I hope you liked it," Margaret said to her therapist. "That truly was inspiring, Maggie," he replied, "Now I hope you understand what you should take from that."

"Yes, sir," she said.

"And what is that?" he asked.

"That I should not let my questions, curiosities, and emotions take over. I should think things through," Margaret answered.

"That's right," he said, "Now go on, and live your life to its greatest potential." "I'm glad we did this, Maggie," Gail said as they walked out, "It's helped both of us return to normal."

"You're welcome, Mom," she said, "you're welcome."

After that, life had returned to its perfection. Margaret grew up and had kids of her own. Gail had started her own bakery and Bill had found a place to lie down and relax.

A Different View of Dark

LAUREL CHILDRESS, 17

W RYN'S FINGER HAD NEVER ONCE STOPPED TAPPING THE whole time she sat on her porch. The same way her eyes never once left her bustling street where people continued on their way, not even sparing her a glance. Made sense, after all, she was only here all the time.

Sitting back, Wryn tossed her head to get a better view of the upstairs window. Mom stood there, already knowing the intentions behind the casual check and sending her a warning glare. Her ever-present eyes monitoring her every move.

Wryn sighed, fingers still tapping. She considered herself a pretty good finger tapper. She'd had plenty of practice.

Weekends were the supposed to be the best part of everyone's days, but not for Wryn. Especially when your parents refuse to let you out of the yard, let alone into town. They lived close, but just far enough away from school and town and everyone that there was just nothing to do.

During these times Wryn spent as much time outside as much, typically people watching. Wondering as neighbors go by, what do they face when they get home?

She's been on lockdown since her last *incident*. She and Ollie had been helping Shen with her new place. Wryn's disappointment in her father's decision when he told her that she couldn't spend time with him cut deep. It didn't matter that Ollie was one of the only kids her age from school that lived nearby. It only mattered Ollie was a boy and "a bad influence".

"You can't go with him anymore," Dad said.

Wryn's jaw tightened at the memory.

Deep down she knew her mom and dad were only trying to keep her safe, but sometimes their attempts to control Wryn's life just got to the point of ridiculousness.

Sneaking away may prove a bit more challenging since her father's declaration, but Wryn was good at waiting.

She sneaked another peek above. Mom was still in front of the window, doing laundry or some other such excuse to be outside and be watching Wryn's every move.

As the dinner hour approached and the sun started its long decline into night, fewer feet were on the street, and as the sounds of busy traffic faded out, Wryn heard the sound of a familiar squeak. The sight of the sleepy boy pulling the wagon made her fingers finally stop tapping.

Novin was probably her best friend, ever since they met during one of his deliveries.

Wryn twirled her hair around indifferently, pretending to not even see her friend. *No one* was at the window. Wryn welcomed whatever distraction that has allowed her to slip out from under her mother's hawk-eyed gaze.

Wryn walked down the porch steps closer to Novin, glancing behind her one more time, walking down the stairs but stopping before she got out of arm's reach of the railing.

"Hey Wryn." Novin wiped a greasy clump of soot-colored hair from his forehead. He smiled lazily and let go of the cart and its familiar blue tarp covering whatever laid inside. Wryn heard a rattling as the contents shifted from the harsh landing.

"Whatcha doing here?" Novin asked, a half-hearted sarcastic smile chasing the comment. "Weren't you helping what's-her-face with something or other?"

"I am currently grounded and completely alone and out of touch with everyone."

He laughed, crossing his arms. "There's nothing keeping you from just walking away," he said calmly.

She scowled back at him. "Don't say that! You don't understand! While I'm stuck here you can go anywhere!"

Wryn glanced sideways, feeling Novin's eyes on her, watching, waiting.

After a moment when she managed to hold out on his silence, Novin chuckled. "She won't be able to stop you if you run fast enough."

Wryn rolled her eyes but huffed at the image all the same. "You know I can't do that!" She said, looking down. "They'd kill me," she said. "Plus, it's not like I currently have anywhere interesting to go if I did run!"

"Ah, you may not, but you do know how to get places. You can let the destination work itself out on the way." Novin's eyes glinted with an emotion Wryn couldn't place, unusual for her, since she'd always been able to read him fairly well.

"Where would I even go?" She questioned out loud, ignoring Novin's prodding.

A breeze blew from the road. Novin turned his head to look, causing his already tangled hair to whip chaotically around his face.

"Well, I guess I'll just be on my way," he said. "After all, I have a delivery to finish, maybe stop around town, see where I may lend a hand."

"Wait!" Wryn let out a choked sound, taking a hesitant step forward. She wanted to go, she really did.

Novin turned back with an expectant look on his face.

"At least..." she hesitated, "At least tell me about where you're going, since I can't come?"

Novin smiled, and if he had put any more effort in, it might have looked a bit mischievous. "Not sure I have enough time..."

Wryn rolled her eyes again. "Fine, I guess it's not that interesting."

"Ok," he replied, "I'm only going to the next town over. It's pretty much the same as here, people trying to make money... people trying to tolerate each other...." He shrugged. "You know, the norm. There's some buildings, a few trees, roads, some have sidewalks and more shops."

"Not fair!" Wryn giggled and pushed his arm.

"Oh no, it is!" He said in a fake wistful way. "You just have to see it to understand." He moved his hand to his forehead dramatically. "Oh the magic! The lives of all those people!" Novin let his hand fall, his signature crooked grin stretching across his face.

Wryn glanced back at the window nervously. Empty. "Maybe I could walk with you to the end of the town?"

Novin raised an eyebrow.

"We're close anyway!" Wryn fumed. "It's not like I'd be going far!"

"Be my guest." Novin picked up his wagon and began to walk down the street, and Wryn walked next to him.

She buzzed with nervous energy. Even if she was only going only to the edge of town and had walked this way before, it was never without one of her parents along.

Novin glanced at her, tilting his head.

"Come on, this isn't that amazing," he said.

Wryn glared at him, and Novin chuckled.

Along the way a few people nodded at Novin in greeting. Novin didn't respond. Wryn wondered if he was even aware they were addressing him.

"I've been meaning to ask you," Wryn started, "Why haven't you been in school."

A dark look passed momentarily over Novin's face. Wryn night have missed it if she hadn't been looking.

"I mean, I've never really seen you there and I just wondered."

Novin shrugged. "School isn't for me. My brother has me running deliveries, plus I already know all I need. The amount people have to pay, what to give them and all."

Wryn tilted her head, searching his face for something. Some revelation about how he felt about being a delivery boy.

"Don't you want to do something more?" Wryn asked. "Or just work for your brother your whole life?"

"Eh, I'm not worried about it." Novin glanced at her nonchalantly. "I'll figure something out."

Wryn looked at him, slightly shocked, and shook her head in disapproval. "If you want to have a worthwhile job you need degrees and qualifications."

"Depending where you want to work," he retorted.

Novin sighed and closed his eyes a moment. "Come on, nowadays no one cares about who said what, when, and you know, whatever? All people wanna know is if you have four working limbs and some common sense. With those, you can get what-ever job you want."

"Not whatever job..." Wryn felt deflated. "If no one went to school, how would anyone become a doctor? Helping other people?"

"I don't know, being smart, I suppose. Eh, it doesn't really matter. I help people in different ways."

Wryn wasn't completely satisfied with this response, but in her mind she had won the argument, so she let the subject drop.

As they passed a tall, ruby house, Wryn glanced at it uneasily. And of course Mrs. Stroem would be outside right now, leaning over her bushes, her eyes burn-ing as she watched them. Mrs. Stroem and her tight, silver-blonde bun was often outside doing yard work, glaring with dissatisfaction at all the people passing. "Ah, what's this?" Mrs. Stroem's shrill voice quipped as they rolled the cart past her property. "The Delbord girl walking with the local delinquent."

Wryn glanced at Novin, who raised his eyebrows. But he ignored her same as the others and contin-ued walking.

Wryn paused, frowning. "It's okay Mrs. Stroem, I'm just helping him to the end of town."

Novin stopped to wait.

Mrs. Stroem scowled at Novin. "Your dad know you're hanging about with him?" she asked, her amber eyes boring into Wryn.

Novin flashed a grin in response.

Wryn chuckled nervously, rubbing her palms. "He's uh... my mom's the only one home. She saw me leave."

That wasn't necessarily untrue. Wryn felt Mrs. Stroem's stares boring into her back as they walked away.

Their town didn't have an official sign or anything that said, 'Now leaving Burnhaven.' There was only a dirt road that marked the boundary and led into the fields beyond. On a clear day, if she squinted, Wryn could see the small blob of another village far off in the distance.

Novin sat down the wagon and turned to Wryn, his hair falling in front of his eyes. He didn't notice, or at least he didn't move it out of the way.

"Well, this is where we must part ways, I'm afraid."

Wryn giggled, then looked at the fields ahead, both quiet for a moment.

Until Novin playfully slapped her head.

Wryn rubbed the spot but grinned at him.

"Maybe next time you can come the whole way," he said. "We could walk there and back in the same day."

Wryn smiled softly before looking out at the road again.

"My parents would never let me without one of them."

Novin shrugged, "It's up to you."

"I expect I'll get an earful cause I left without telling, especially because I wasn't supposed to go anywhere. I don't think I want to find out what would happen I left town all together and they found out."

"Just saying it'd be easy to say you're hanging out with one of your friends doing homework or something. With your track record, I doubt they'd suspect a thing."

Novin picked the wagon back up, both of them ignoring the slightly alarming creaking sound it made. "Not that I know anyhow..." Novin said.

Wryn frowned slightly.

"Well, I gotta get going. See ya later and all that."

Wryn said her goodbyes and couldn't help but watch him for a bit longer, her hands fidgeting. He turned back and she waved. He smiled and continued on.

What could she say to her parents? They say again and again that they knew what was best. Although they occasionally had their issues, she was good enough that her parents wouldn't question any excuse she might give. Novin wasn't exactly wrong. But a twisting feeling of guilt raised up in her chest at the thought of lying to them.

It would be so easy...

Sighing, she turned around and started back the way she'd come. There was always another day.

Cold Classrooms and Empty Promises—
Observations in Verse

LAUREL CHILDRESS, 17

Spoken Word

The two ingredients to the world's most deadly poison,
and yet I still dive right in.

Cold Classrooms,

Filled to the brim with teenage hearts.
      I enter.
Sneaking stares while the other isn't looking,
Wishful thinking of things that never happened,
I use my hand to keep my pen warm
Because how else am I expected to believe what they
tell us?
That there's more and it's better and that we'll be
better?
Unless the ink in my pen freezes before I can take
notes.

Hate with a side of judgment,
The world's second most deadly poison.
The mind of a teenage girl
Sprinkle in some false joy and smarts to make sure
people can't recognize it
at first glance. Empty Promises,
Promises to watch the stars in the summer.
Promises to get grades up
Promises to tell the other the truth.
They tell us it doesn't matter as long as the heart was
in the right place.
The world's empty promise to us.

> Teenage hearts and teenage minds in cold
> classrooms.

Cold classrooms overflowing with empty promises,
> The promise you gave me while sitting on a tall
> table that makes me question being with you in
> those cold classrooms.

The promise I gave you.
But as every day passes, I find myself questioning
more and more if I can really make it somehow more
than just one of our empty promises.
Call me a snake
Call me the one who got away
I don't care.
Call me a liar
Call me a fool.

I'll still somehow fall for your tricks no matter
how many times you break me. I'll spill my guts onto
these pages and feel how the words taste on my lips,
But I'll never speak them out loud.
My feels written between the lines of music and fake
texts instead.
Call me horrible.
Call me untrustworthy.
> There's nothing you say that I haven't already
> thought about you.
Spin your lies-not lies into my life, making it too
painful for me to rip out. I can read your eyes.
I know you call me a leech.
My tongue will roll around those words I'm itching to
say.
Call me loving.
Call me funny.
> Only because I know you sneak glances at me
> when you think I'm not
> looking. Red fingers and god-awful texts.
An untrustworthy friend and the one who got away.
Boiling guts and liars.
A fool and a truck load of snakes.
> Take your pick love.

Sometimes I wish I could just disappear in the crack
between my bed and the wall. The cold and the
pressure in that small safe place tempting.
Kinder than the heat radiating from the dogs next to
me
Softer than the bit of cold air coming from an open
window in the middle of
the night. A place I can simply think of all that's to be
done,
But make no move to do them.

   Maybe the people would forget I was there,
The different words and personalities clashing
together.
But for once I wouldn't need to be in between.

    Being away for even five minutes writing this I
    can feel the knots in my brain
    loosening. Imagine what being able to stay in
    that crack might feel like.
Maybe everything I know can be forgotten.
My brain might finally able to relax.
Instead of constantly running on my fears, doubts,
and the things still left to
be done. Stuck between the wall and my bed.
Everything out of my control.
Maybe, while stuck staring at the crack of ceiling still
visible,
I could finally understand why I laugh when they don't,
Why I fail when they win,

Why for some reason I try to convince myself it is up to me, and
me alone, To do what everyone else chooses to forget.

Write Me a Song

I hold a pen in my hand
It drips onto the paper by itself
I don't even have to write anything
The ink spells out words and worlds I can only see in my mind
Help me make it through my day
The ink stains my fingers and mind
Makes me feel like I'm somewhere else
A place where ink folds new worlds out of thin air
And I'm not here, but far away hidden in a forgotten dream.
It spells out songs and stories that others won't recognize.
With water and trees and animals and me
I wish it could take me with
Somewhere else, where ink folds new worlds
And the only problems are those of heroes.
And a day is never wasted.
And I can do things I know I could never do here.

I hold a pen in my hand.
It knits together words without me even writing.

Take me far away to a hidden dream.
Help me make it through my day.
Silence is Deafening
I don't want to just play it safe
But an overwhelming fear floods my every bone, my
every muscle, my
entire being Thoughts slam against my skull making it
hard to breathe

> *They hate you*
> *Why would they ever want to be by you?*
> *What did you do wrong this time?*

They claw at me raking my wrists as crimson
liquid bleeds through my invisible wounds as I try
desperately to cover them up.
Words threaten to roll out of my mouth from behind
my tongue, making everyone around turn to look at
me weirdly.
Making them turn to stare.
Making them turn to leave.
My mind boils over like two armies firing bullets at
each other crying out in pain. I let them lodge the
bullets between my brain and blood and keep me
awake thinking. Keeping me from sleeping
Keeping me from speaking my mind
My feet ache as I attempt to stumble through my day.
Sending glances at people who I wish would take the
time to see inside
my head. See the mold growing up the sides of my

skull, suffocating my
feelings and words. The words I wish I could say to
them.
The words I wish they could ever be able to
understand.
And people ask why I'm always tired.
You sat with half empty glasses of orange juice on your
bed stand, untouched.
You don't bother to move it.
Next to it is a cup of pens.
That somehow have written themselves into your life.
Red for the bleeding hearts you've experienced,
blue for the cold and dark nights much like this one,
and bright pink for the friends and lovers who you've
let into your life.
They remind you of all those creations and loves that
you've left unfinished,
the disappointment in your father's eyes.
The demons in the living room chasing you away,
causing you to wrap yourself up in the safety of your
room, your cage.
The room that has somehow become so much and so
little at the same time.
With stars laced out in the dry and empty air that has
become more of a home to you than the rest of this
house ever had been.

You sit on the bed, remembering how the feeling
of warmth you experienced under its sheets had so
quickly turned clammy, became unwanted.
Just like that empty glass of orange juice sitting next
to you.
So many dreams lost and stored away inside these
thin walls
Where you easily hear your sister, her tears and cries
throughout the night.
But I don't worry, she's flown away now.

The longer you stay in this room, the more it chokes
you.
You remembering the stories you've created
That have come from these terrifying four walls.
Stories left unfinished.
Broken ideas forever a part of you,
Carried with you wherever you go.
Constantly reminding you how much there is to lose.

The pink pen, the red, the blue, the purple, the green,
the black, and the yellow. All left visible on your hands
and computer. Smeared with drop less of black and
blue.
Stars and dots crisscrossed on your shoes and in your
eyes.
What more would you ask for?

What more than the stars in your eyes and the ink on your hands?
Surely not the best friend, the love that you lost all those days ago. Not the care and family you once had before it disappeared. Not the understanding of a disappointed father and the love of a living aunt. Not the heart of someone who knows and understands these nights of dying laughter. Not the piece of your heart that can never seemed to be filled.

These stories are all left unfinished.

Listen to your heart, they tell you. But your heart has stopped working a long time ago. Now the only thing left to lead you is the empty echo of something that was once wonderful and beautiful. A heart bursting with life and love, that is now gone, dead along with the galaxies in your eyes. But you have your pens, you have your bed. You have your room and you have your body. There's nothing more that you need.

You're left wondering why in a stuffy room.
I can see how your hands barely keeping from shaking,
Left wondering why.
There are so many things circling in your head
Despite what everyone keeps saying.

You wish the monster which was once under your bed
would talk to you again.
Even if it was just to bite and scratch.

Because then you would know that it wasn't just you
who cared.
Even if you only wanted it gone, and hated how it
made you feel so lonely and used every night. You
wanted to know that all of your suspicions were
wrong, that the monster cared for you even if it was
just for a food source.
Because after a while you realize that the monster was
the one who managed to make you fall in love with
this pain and hurt. The reason why your hands want
so desperately to shake.

But your hands are shaking and you're avoiding that
bed because you know deep down it didn't care for
you. You know deep down you aren't wondering a
thing. Because you already know. You just wish it
wasn't true.
You just want to know that somewhere in that monster
there is still the heart of a human. A human who feels
sorrow for hurting you and feels regret for scarring
your heart with teeth marks. That there was some part
of that monster who loved you.
But you have suspicions.

And so far, even the worse of those suspicions have
been proven right.

But there's nothing.
You did the right thing.
You chased the monster out.
But now you would just wish it would knock at your
window asking to be let in. That maybe somehow that
monster had gotten attached to you. Attached to the
underside of your bed, and maybe it didn't want to
leave.
Instead you're left wishing it wasn't true,
And with a new batch of multicolored pens sitting on
the nightstand, beside you.

Agave

ANNALIESE AI GUMBOC, 17

I WAS BORN AT THE ADVENT OF AUTUMN, IN THE SIXTH YEAR of the New Age, as the wrath of summer dissipated at the soothing touch of the wind; as Demeter despaired the loss of her daughter; as the stars rearranged to enshrine the deeds of Perseus. I am told it was a clear night, the entirety of the Milky Way spilling across the sky, the waning moon casting dim light from her seat in the heavens. A breeze danced in the soft glow of night, weaving through crumbling buildings, narrow streets, and abandoned cars, stirring leaves of scarlet and gold. The constellation Andromeda shone brightly above the city of Thebes as I was brought into the world.

They named me Agave.

My father was Cadmus, the king of Thebes. My mother was Harmonia, Cadmus' second wife, a beautiful young woman with fair hair and milk-white skin. I was not Cadmus' firstborn child but was his first to survive past the age of one. Thus, in my toddlerhood, he treated me with great love and attention, and in turn, I adored him.

By the time I was four, Harmonia had borne Cadmus two more girls, Ino and Autonoe. My sisters and I shared the same features: our mother's bright eyes and ivory skin, our father's dark hair. We were inseparable from the beginning, together romping the halls of our father's villa. We had free rein of the house, so long as we avoided sunlight—our mother feared it would ruin our complexions.

Cadmus' villa was located in the southeast corner of Thebes, on a gentle slope overlooking the rest of the city, which poured from the hillside onto a green plain. My sisters and I spent much of our time on the highest floor of the house, from where we could see the sprawl of Thebes: white buildings with clay roofs, winding streets lined with lamps and utility posts—remnants of a bygone era. Beyond the city walls, farmland stretched in all directions, interrupted by the web of roads extending out of Thebes. To the east lay the river of

Ismeneus, and to the west, the river of Dirce, the two converging in the north. On a clear day, we could make out the peaks of Kithairon in the far distance, a hazy shadow sitting low on the southwest horizon. We marveled at such sights, for we had never traveled past the fortifications of Thebes.

I once asked my father why women were forbidden from going beyond the city walls, while men left regularly to hunt and farm. Cadmus had chuckled. "Like Deucalion and Pyrrha, the gods have spared us for our piety, and now we must repopulate the desolate earth. Women are made to give birth, so we must keep them safe–they are our most important commodity."

Cadmus ensured that my sisters and I received an education, particularly in the history of the gods. However, it was our mother who taught us the most important skill for a girl to possess: weaving. She showed us how to place our hands, how to set the staves of the loom, to weave the weft through the warp. We tried at first with clumsy hands, tangling the cheap, undyed yarn that had been given to us for practice. But we learned from our mistakes, and gradually, our movements grew steadier and assured.

We spent every day in the women's sitting room, weaving, usually creating clothes, as those were a necessity. Sometimes we started from scratch, and sometimes we repurposed strange clothing leftover from the late Iron Age. Harmonia–who had been a teenager at the end of the Iron Age—would occasionally point to an article and say, "I used to wear these all the time." I couldn't imagine her wearing anything but a white peplos.

Harmonia would sing while we worked, her voice resembling the highest chords of a lyre. I cherished this time, as it was one of the few activities we did with our mother. But our routine was soon disrupted by Harmonia's enlarged stomach, which seemed to grow more rapidly each day. Within a few months, she was so heavy with child that she could hardly stand, let alone weave at the loom.

When the time came for the baby to arrive, a midwife brought me to my mother's bedside. "You are seven now," my mother said to me. "It is time that you learn such things."

I remained by Harmonia's side through the entire ordeal, witnessing her labored breaths and painful cries. The thing that came out was screaming and red and covered in bodily fluids. A midwife swaddled the infant tightly in cloth and handed it to my mother. Harmonia was uncharacteristically uncollected, her eyes heavy-lidded, her fair hair wet and matted. The infant quieted as she cradled it to her chest, murmuring words too soft for me to hear.

The room seemed to tense when my father entered.

"A boy this time?" he asked as he crossed the threshold of the room.

Harmonia hesitated, then answered, "No. A girl." Her voice was coarse and exhausted.

A charged silence filled the air. Cadmus inhaled deeply, the anger clear on his face. He spoke through gritted teeth. "When will you give me an heir?"

"I'm trying."

"Not hard enough," he snapped. And with that, he left.

Later, the infant was named Semele.

The New Age festival—a ten-day celebration honoring the beginning of the New Age—was one of the few times per year that my sisters and I were permitted to go out into the city of Thebes. Most days, we were confined to the villa. It was an adventure for us—we were fascinated by the artifacts scattered throughout the city, from confusing metal contraptions to signs boasting phrases like "Viofos Lighting." Most of the festival's events took place at either the ruins of the Cadmea or the Archaeological Museum of Thebes, where my father had worked. There, he would stand before our people and recite the story of how he had foreseen the end of the Iron Age and saved Thebes from destruction.

"I was taking a walk one summer afternoon when I was suddenly overcome by a wave of heat and light. I fell to the ground, and a booming voice cried out from above—it was Apollo himself. He proclaimed that the gods would soon wipe out mankind and begin civilization anew, as the ways and virtues of the ancients had nearly been lost. He ordered me to go out and share my knowledge, for those who reverted to the old ways would be saved."

"So I did as I had been commanded...but no one believed me. They laughed at me, called me a madman. I lost my job. But what I predicted came to pass. A plague began in Mesopotamia and spread around the globe, killing almost all it touched."

"As the disease swept through Greece, the people saw that my words were true. Soon, people throughout Boeotia flocked to Thebes to hear my teachings. I taught them the history of the gods; I taught them to use ancient tools from the museum. And when the plague arrived in Thebes, it spared the true believers."

"Together, we brought back the ancient ways, recreated ancient tools, built farms, tore down buildings to reconstruct the walls of Thebes."

"Then came the End. At the dusk of the plague's third anniversary, brilliant auroras streaked across the sky. Every electronic device emitted a bevy of sparks, then died. Thus began the New Age."

The week I turned thirteen, I was married to Echion—a brutish man, twenty years my elder, and one of my father's favorite soldiers. He had no children, no servants; it was just the two of us in his empty house.

I spent most of my days alone, in the house's women's room, weaving, weaving, weaving.

It was not the same as when I had done so as a child, with my sisters beside me, my mother's melodious voice lifting to fill the room. Instead, I worked in stifling silence as the sparsely decorated walls of the room closed in. I kept the windows open, but this did little to alleviate my feelings of claustrophobia. I could only mark the passage of time by the changing of shadows in the room and the progression of the cloth on the loom.

The days became indistinguishable, each following the same course, like a weft thread repeatedly winding through the warp. My life was trapped in a circle, going round and round and leading nowhere at all.

I was eighteen when I felt my first child kicking within my womb. I thanked Hera for it, for Echion had grown dangerously frustrated with his lack of children. Delivering the child was as painful and difficult as I had feared, but all of that was forgotten once I held my infant son in my arms. At first, my senses were overwhelmed with emotion, some mixture of love and elation too powerful to properly articulate. Then, I realized the significance of what I had just done: I had borne a son. My father now had a male descendant—in my arms, I held the future king of Thebes.

The people of Thebes celebrated, and I basked in the glory, knowing I had done my duty well—yet, there was an underlying sadness I could not escape.

Pentheus—as I named my son—became the center of my life. I watched with pride as he grew into a little boy with wild hair and a wide grin. When it came time for his education, I took charge, teaching him his basics and hiring the best tutors in Thebes for further instruction.

I did not have any children after Pentheus, but Echion and Cadmus did not seem to mind—one son was worth more than four daughters.

Semele was only fourteen when she died in childbirth. Cadmus mourned her death, for her infant son died only hours later. As I watched men lower my little sister into her grave, all I could think was: That could have been me.

As the years passed, Pentheus transformed from a toddling boy into a young man who had his mother's eyes, his father's ill-temper, and an immovable resolve that I prided myself in teaching him. With a suitable heir, my aging father was finally able to pass on the mantle of king.

I had thought being the mother of the king would somehow make things better for me, but it did not.

Pentheus did not need his mother anymore—a fact he made very clear, brushing off any attempt I made to advise or assist him. He moved into my father's villa, which was now his own, leaving me alone in the house of Echion. I visited friends and family as often as I could, but the periods in between these brief hours were filled with crushing monotony and loneliness.

I spent the days mostly weaving, caged in by the walls of the house. Life returned to the same miserable cycle that I had endured before having Pentheus. I had aged considerably since then and was now approaching my forties, and yet my life was still the same—I had never even ventured beyond the walls of the city.

Almost forty, and I have hardly lived at all. This thought prompted anger, but that was lost to an overwhelming sense of sadness. This is what my life would amount to, I realized: a pile of weavings.

Cloaked by darkness and clothed in a himation, I carefully open the southwestern gate, located in a quiet corner of Thebes. There is no one guarding the city walls—though once enforced, that practice had progressively relaxed as the years passed without any sign of a serious external threat.

I pause at the threshold of the gate, in awe of the sight before me. Fields roll out in every direction to meet the night at the horizon, the landscape and its features silhouetted against a bright, star-streaked sky. An asphalt road, overcome with cracks and weeds, extends through the gate and continues southward, snaking towards the peaks of Kithairon. It is a world impossibly wide, uninterrupted by walls.

A gust of autumn wind sweeps in from the south, whipping through my hair and clothes, carrying the scent of freshly harvested grapes. It howls like an animal, wild and free, urging me onward. My heart races as my desires war with everything I've been taught. I draw a deep breath, then take my first step past the walls of Thebes.

Feeling an intoxicating rush of exhilaration, I laugh as I take another step, then another, then soon I'm running down the road, stretching my legs in a way I've never done before. I pass buildings and fields—some abandoned, some not—and do not stop until I reach the edge of Theban farmland. The last farmhouse teeters on the precipice of the unknown, distinguished from the shadows by lamplight spilling from a sole window.

I turn back to look at Thebes, only to find that everything I've ever known has already been reduced to a hub of distant lights. I cannot go back—I would rather face the beasts and trials of the wild than spend another day trapped inside. So instead, I look forward: to Andromeda, gazing down from above, and to Kithairon, its shadow calling me forth to explore a vast new world.

Nightmare School

ABIGAIL M. HULL, 11

I AM A 16 YEAR OLD GIRL. MY NAME IS ISABEL, MY BEST FRIEND Lila and I go to River High. I have straight blonde hair with beach tan skin. Everything was perfect.

I had friends.

Lila and I had sleepovers every weekend until, one day when they got on the bus there were two new boys Anthony, and Luke, they taunted me saying "Hey, you! Girl you should go to a beauty salon and fix your hair."

"Back off" Lila said.

"Hey, miss pretty, sit down with me and let's talk" Anthony said.

"No, Mr. Twinkle toes," she snarled. "Watch what you say to Anthony" said Luke

"Why?" she asked sitting down next to me.

"Because he has his ways" Luke said with an evil grin on his face

"What, is he going to charm me?" Lila said, rolling her eyes, smirking. The boys fell silent.

"Thanks Lila" I Whispered.

"No problem" she answered.

"I don't know what I would do without you Lila" I said sadly.

"You don't need me, protect yourself." They just got to school, and they got off the bus. Anthony gave me a punch to the back.

"Ow!" I shrieked.

"What was that about" Lila yelled.

"She is ugly" Anthony said.

"No, she is not, you're ugly" Lila yelled, throwing her beautiful blonde hair.

"Ouch!" Anthony said Looking very hurt.

"If you're so good at offense then you should work on defense," Lila said, grining. Anthony fell down. Luke ran over and tried to punch Lila, she caught his fist and "You cannot punch me" Lila snarled.

"Ow" he screamed.

"Not so tough now, huh" Lila said. Walking toward the school, with me right behind her. Then Lila starts coughing and falls to the floor.

"Help! Someone help! Lila is sick! Help!" I shrieked.

"I am coming!" called the school nurse.

"Thank you!" I said.

"Get her to my office now" said Mrs. Smith the school nurse.

"Okay," I said, grabbing Lila and bringing her to the Nurse Office.

Mrs. Smith walked after me and screamed "get away from her."

Isabel jumped back in horror "What, what is wrong?"

Mrs. Smith answered "She has a lung disease that is contagious."

"That's terrible, I will call her parents," I said, worried for my friend.

I ran over to the telephone and dialed her mom's number. "Hello, Mrs. King I am in the nurse's office because I helped Mrs. Smith take Lila here she has a contagious lung disease and we are sending her to the closest hospital. Please meet us there."

"Okay, I will be there in thirty minutes thank you for telling me, bye-bye" and she hung up.

Then I called 991.

"Hello we are at River High a girl named Lila King has come down with a very contagious lung disease. Please help."

The person on the other side of the phone said, "Yes okay, will be there in three minutes."

Three minutes later...

Isabel heard a siren blare and she ran out of the school waving her yelling "over here!"

They saw her get out of the vehicle and followed her into the school.

"In here," she said pointing.

Then she walked away feeling that she played a big part in helping her friend.

I ran into my friend May, "Hey, is Lila okay?" May asked.

"No, we need help, is your mom working today?" I replied.

"Yes, why?" May asked.

I gave her an annoyed expression "She can drive us to the Hospital!" I said frustrated.

"Oh, yeah sure sorry" May said apologetically and she ran toward the office, "Mom" she called.

"Yes," Ms. Nicole answered, coming up to the door.

"Lila had to go to the hospital, can you please drive us there?" May pleaded.

"Oh, my god! Let's go!" She ran out of her office, "Isabel, get in the car!"

"Yes. Ma'am" I said, chasing after Ms. Nicole and getting into the car. Twenty minutes later they got to hospital.

"Hurry up" said Ms. Nicole, walking into the hospital while we followed her and then I ran into Anthony and Luke.

"Where are you going," Anthony taunted

"Wherever I am checking on Lila, and why do you care Anth-puppy" I replied.

"Watch what you say to me" Anthony snarled, glaring at me.

"Why?" I asked

"Because if not I will find a way to take Lila away from you forever," He replied, his voice as cold as ice, a sly grin crossing his face.

"She would not leave me to go with you," I replied with fire burning in my throat, "Good Day!" I said.

"You would be surprised," he said angrily. Then growled deep in his throat.

"Why are you even here?" I ask suspiciously.

"I came to my sister" Luke said. "Anthony came to see Lila."

"Do you and Lila have such a great love? I don't think so. She hates you." I started to walk away then spun around and punched Anthony in the face to find out he was a robot "Wh-wh-what" I stammered.

Luke looked as shocked as I felt. After school that day I realized I never want to see a robot again and before dinner that night I grabbed a notebook, a magnifying glass, and put it in my school Bag. I put on dark blue pald pj's, brushed my teeth, and went to bed.

The next day I got dressed in a white blouse and a dark red shirt with silver flat shoes. Then I went downstairs to eat pancakes with strawberries, after breakfast I went to brush my teeth, and then I grabbed my homework, put it in my backpack and left for River High.

"I am going to find whoever did this" I whispered to myself and got on the bus.

"Hey, Luke," I said and sat down next to him being nice because of what Anthony was.

"Hey, Isabel," He said, moving over in the seat.

"How are you?" I said, "Good, how about you?" Luke said.

"Um, nervous. I am going to find whoever is controlling Anthony the robot" I said nervously.

"Oh, can I help" Luke said

"Sure," I said, as the bus stopped at the school.

"Let's go!" Luke said, getting up and walking out of the bus.

"Coming," I said, following Luke and grabbing a notepad from my backpack.

"Where do we start?" Luke asked.

"Umm, we should ask around, or look in the phone book for where he lived" I said, catching up to Luke.

"I will ask around, you should look in the phone book" Luke said.

"Okay, we will meet back here after school. Then figure it all out, got it?" I said

"Yep," Luke said, walking towards the 10th grade math class.

I ran towards the eleventh grade language arts, "Ssorry, I am late Mr. Litan" I said.

"It is okay" Mr. Litan said. "Sit down."

"Okay, Mr. Litan," I said, sitting down at the back of the class.

"Everybody take out your notebooks please," Mr. Litan said.

"Yes, Mr. Litan" Everyone said in unison.

"Open to page seventy-two, chapter three" Mr. Litan said.

"Mr. Litan um, Can I go to the bathroom?" I said.

"Yes, Isabel," Mr. Litan said.

"Thank you, Mr. Litan" I said and walked away.

"You're welcome," Mr. Litan said.

I walked towards the door and mumbled, "I need to get a student phone book." I ran toward my locker, typed in the code 4893 and opened my locker and grabbed my student hand book.

"Um, what are you doing?" My friend May asked from behind me.

"I think Anthony the robot was the one that made Lila very sick and I am going to figure out who was controlling Anthony" I said.

"Oh, Can I help?" May asked.

"Um, you can try?" I said.

"Thanks! He's last name is Hilo" May said.

"Anthony Hilo," I said looking at the phone book.

"Look," May said pointing at the Address 9851 Ocean Way under the name Anthony Hilo.

"Oh, my god!!" I whispered, looking down after Anthony Hilo's name was the name of a man named Carter Hilo with a different address.

"You have a lead," May said, seeing the name.

"Yup, I can't wait until we tell Luke" I said with excitement.

"You're working with Luke?" May asked.

"Yes, why?" I asked.

"Um, he was the best quote on quote friend," May said.

"He is kind and I kind of like him," I said.

"Oh, you *love* him," May said.

"No" I said sharply "I have to get back to class"

"Oh, goodbye" she said.

I ran towards my classroom, "I'm back Mr. Litan, sorry I took so long," I said.

"That's okay" Mr. Litan said, "Get to work."

"Yes, sir," I said and finished the work in twenty-five minutes and heard the bell ring.

"Good day students," Mr. Litan said.

All the students rushed out of the classroom.

"May, Luke, let's have lunch at the beach," I said.

"Ok!" They answered in unison.

"Follow me!" I said.

"Great! What are you guys having for lunch?" I said.

"I am having a Caesar salad and croutons," May said.

"I am having a tuna fish sandwich with blood orange, what are you having?" Luke asked.

"I'm having a fruit salad and some pasta," I said.

When they got there they sat down and unpacked their lunches.

"When we looked in the phone book we saw there was a boy named Carter Hilo has the same last name as Anthony but, lives in a different address" I said.

"Oh, That's great!" Luke said happily.

"We have to go to the house of that person," I said.

"Yup, let's go. We have one hour before we have to get back to school, come on," May said. They ran towards the street and down the avenue towards Dolphin Way.

"Come one," I said. I put on a burst of speed, turned into a driveway and my friends followed me.

Luke banged on the door "Hello anyone home?" He called.

"Hello, my name is Carter," Carter said.

"I am Isabel, this is May, and that is Luke" I said.

"What school do you go to?" Carter asked.

"River High," We said in unison.

"Oh, my god go away!!!" Carter said.

"No!" Luke yelled, putting his foot in the door.

"Go away," Carter yelled, pushing Luke's foot out of the door frame, and slammed the door.

"Let's sneak in through the window over there," May said, pointing to an office window. We nodded and followed her ducking down so Carter could see us.

"I'll go first" I said, getting a boost from Luke and snuck through the window and helped May into the office.

We each grabbed one of Luke's arms and pulled him through the window "Ow!" He exclaimed because he bumped his head.

"Shh!!" we whispered at him, and they heard footsteps coming.

"Hide!" I said, diving behind the bookcases. I saw Luke dive under the desk and saw May hide behind a plant.

"I hope those kids left," He muttered to himself, sitting down in his chair by his desk. Luke grabbed the duct tape on the desk and taped Carter's legs to the floor and desk.

"Ahh!!!!" Carter screamed and May, Luke, and I jumped out, up, or around.

"We know you programmed Anthony" We yelled in unison, glaring at him like we could kill him with our eyes .

"Fine! Yes, I made Anthony the robot and made Lila get sick" Carter yelled.

I grabbed my phone and called 911 "Hello I found the person who made Lila sick" I said

"Thank you" said the lady and 5 minutes later Carter was in a police car and was gone.

Then I called Mrs. King. "Mrs. K we found who hurt your daughter and they're going to jail." I said, then waited for her answer.

"That's amazing thank you! When is my daughter going to heal and be ready to go back to school?" She asked.

"She should be back to school by tomorrow morning" I said happily.

That Night I went to the hospital and told Lila all about it. Lila was so impressed she said "I guess you don't need my help".

"No, I don't think so" I said, "But it is still great to have you!"

"Oh, I know," Lila said, smiling. "Look behind you Isabel," Lila whispers.

I turn around and I see Luke, "hi," he said not looking into my eyes "are you feeling better Lila" he asked.

"Yes, thanks for asking," She said, getting up, hugging him, and whispering, so Luke could hear her "Don't hide that you love Isabel."

He looked at her surprise written all over his face.

"H-h-how?" he asked.

"What??" I said I was confused.

Lila nodded and walked out to get a snack.

"Umm... Isabel, I really like you" Luke says

"Me, too" I answered, then I kissed him and walked out.

"I told you," Lila said.

"You were right!" Luke said, running after me "do you want to go some time?" Luke asks me.

I have a one word answer "Yes!"

The next day Lila came back to school.

The Case of the Missing Fish

EDEN HOLLEMANS, 16

The Case of the Missing Fish - My Journal

Wednesday. 10/1/18

My name is Lola and today was the saddest day of my life. I experienced the worst thing you could ever go through. I will find out what happened to my Fish. Well, I already kinda know but I am definitely not ready to write that down. Writing stuff down makes everything seem so much more real even when I am writing Fantasy stories.

Thursday. 10/5/18

I go to the police station a lot. The police refuse to help me find my Fish and just turn me away because they think it isn't important to find him. I disagree. I really think it is important to find him because he is my Fish. I refuse to have a funeral for him because I know he is still alive. I can feel his presence around me.

Friday. 10/6/18

Today I stayed in my room and cried. I haven't been to school since the accident. My parents think I am going to school but I'm really just staying in my room. My parents think that my Fish isn't important and they try to force me to go to school. No one understands what happened to my Fish, not even my friends. They will never understand.

Saturday. 10/7/18

I have known my Fish for a year and a half or maybe more. I know he likes to swim. My Fish was always in the water. Anytime we hung out it was me watching him swim. I would talk to him and he would listen. Yet, he still had time to care for me. Today, my friends went to the mall and hung out for hours. They invited me but I wasn't ready to go to the mall. There is a pet store there where I met my Fish. I was alone the whole day.

Sunday. 10/8/18

Writing down my thoughts really helps me cope with what happened to my Fish. I went to church today. We had a special time where we could go on stage and share something happy or sad that has happened to us recently. I went up on stage and shared about me losing my Fish. This was a very big thing for me to do. I usually don't speak in front of crowds. I cried almost the whole time. Then I went home and felt way better because I talked about what happened to my Fish even though I don't know much.

Monday. 10/9/18

I told my parents today that I hadn't been going to school and that I was ready to go today. They were happy I told them the truth and that I was ready to go but then they grounded me for the rest of the week. Not like I was planning on going anywhere anyways. School was pretty good today. My friends were being very nice but they were acting like I was a baby some of the time.

Tuesday. 10/10/18

School was terrible today. My so-called "friends" ignored me but when they did talk to me they said they couldn't hang out with me because I was the person that stayed home because I lost my Fish. They said they would get made fun of if they hung out with me. Also, they told me I was going to get made fun of, which happened. Several people called me a cry baby but that didn't affect me. I won't let it. I let my feelings out, now I have to keep them in.

Wednesday. 10/11/18

Today at school I was pushed out of the way a lot. They pushed me like I was trash. Then after school I told my parents what was happening at school. They knew I was still in a slightly fragile state so they comforted me. After they thought I was asleep I heard my mom on the phone with my principal. My mom is the nicest person in the world.

Thursday. 10/12/18

My dad shut my alarm off this morning and let me stay in bed for as long as I wanted. I ended up sleeping until 4pm. My dad was home when I woke up. Usually he works until 7pm and misses dinner. When I asked why he was home he told me to sit down because we needed to talk. I was very worried. He told me that I am going to switch schools because the school wasn't going to do anything about how the other kids were treating me. I am overjoyed. I always hated my school and my friends were only my friends because I paid every time we went out for lunch, dinner, or breakfast. It didn't matter which one.

Friday. 10/13/18

I start my new school on Monday. My new school is right across the street from my house. Originally my parents wanted me to go to my new school but I didn't want to switch at the time. Now, I am fine with switching. I stayed home today because technically I don't go to that school anymore. Now that school is just my old school, nothing more.

Saturday. 10/14/18

I went on a visit to my new school this morning. What I didn't know was that this was the school my Fish went to. My Fish never told me about his life in school. He kept that to himself and shared his feelings and things about him, not what he did with his life, other than swimming. The way I knew this was his school was because I saw a memorial right inside the door. I wanted to scream and tell the office ladies that he is still alive. But I would have no proof other than that I can feel him next to me all the time. The school was great and perfect for me, I guess.

Sunday. 10/15/18

Today my parents let me stay home from church because my dad saw the memorial for Fish and he just knew that it hit me hard. I love my parents: they are so supportive. I stayed in my room for the most part of the day. The only time I was out of my room was when I was eating my breakfast, lunch, and dinner. While I was in my room I was just mentally preparing myself to go to my Fish's old school and have to deal with the hate for seeing the memorial. What is also stressful is being the new kid and not having friends.

Monday. 10/16/18

My first day of school went ok. Everyone was silent in the halls. No one talked to anyone, not even the teachers. At break I heard three people talking and they were all teachers in the lunchroom. I decided to listen in because I had nothing better to do; so I stood right by the door out of view and leaned onto the wall. They were talking about me and how I was new to the school. I listened for a couple more minutes and heard them talk about my Fish. This made me curious but the bell rang so I had to get to class. The rest of the day no one talked other than the teachers teaching their lessons.

Tuesday. 10/17/18

I have a curiosity that kills so today at break I went to the lunchroom door and heard the same three teachers talking. They were talking about Fish! I leaned in more to get a better view of who was talking. All they talked about the whole time I was there was how they still thought my Fish was alive and that gave me more hope. The rest of the day doesn't really matter because nothing important happened. I was very happy throughout the rest of the day.

Wednesday. 10/18/18

At school today everyone was talking in the halls. It was almost like a tsunami of energy washed over them and gave them life. I went to talk to a girl who was by herself (because no one should be left alone). She started talking to me right when I said hello. Her name is Autumn, and she told me that they found my Fish!! I couldn't say anything. I don't know how she knew but she then told me the principal was looking for me. I walked inside and went to the principal's office and he told me the news. He said that my Fish was back but the principal said that he isn't alive.

Sunday. 10/22/18

I am sorry I took a break from writing. I couldn't handle looking at everything I wrote. I had so much faith that he was alive but all of that came crashing down when the principal told me that he thinks Fish is dead.

Monday. 10/23/18

He's gone. No. He can't be. He has to be alive. Everything I have done was for him. The crash, the shooting, the killing. I did it all for him and someone took him away from me. He wouldn't leave. They must've taken him. Keeping me trapped in here as if I wouldn't figure out what they are hiding. I'll figure it out and I'll free him.